CLOUDBURST

RICKY DALE

Published by Ricky Dale
Publishing partner: Paragon Publishing, Rothersthorpe
First published 2019
© Ricky Dale 2019

ISBN 978-1-78222-704-5

Book design, layout and production management by Into Print
www.intoprint.net
+44 (0)1604 832149

This book is for:

Kim who inspired it
Dahlia who discovered it
Sandra who revived it
Mom for her faith

CONTENTS

Part

1: Triumvirate 17

2: Cherchez La Femme. 27

3: Between Mirrors 30

4: Amour Propre 33

5: Reminiscence. 35

6: Favara Brotherhood 42

7: The Voices 45

8: Enigmatic Food For Thought. 48

9: Cum Granulo Salis 49

10: A Curious Journey. 51

11: The Castigation. 53

12: Omerta 54

13: Tick, Tock, Tick. 55

14: Romanticheroic. 57

15: Too Much Pontification! 60

16: Fellow Kooshdakhaa. 62

17: We Joined The Wild Birds In Their Crying. . . . 69

18: Sexuality And The Killing Of Folk. 71

19: Memory Is A Cemetery 74

20: Dangerous Dan McDrew 78

21: Lyonnaise Potatoes. 81

22: Otto, Make That Riff Staccato 84

23: Nice Girls Don't Stay For Breakfast 86

Contents contd./

Part

24: Aaron Slick From Punkin Crick! 90

25: Double Entendre (Entarndra). 93

26: Shanghai Lil. 96

27: It's A Rainy Night (In Georgia) 99

28: What Is A Totemic Occurrence? 110

29: Funny How Blood Stains 114

30: Send In The Fools – 'Clowns'. 116

31: Contagion. 121

32: 'Oh Foi-De-Roi' Shanghai Lillian.. 126

33: Deigratia (By The Grace Of God). 130

34: I Can Still Smell The Fields of Tobacco 132

35: Butterfly Mornings 138

36: Annabel Lee And Me! 140

37: Lucky 'Lemonade' Lucy 148

38: A Deal With The Devil. 154

39: Plastic Silverspoons 156

40: A Phrase Of Love. 160

41: I Did; I Do. 165

42: Stardust.. 169

43: Pianissimo 174

44: Eschewal 181

Chapter 1: Paternity. 185

Addendum. 193

Ricky Dale, A Profile 197

FOREWORD

Is THIS THE greatest semi-autobiographical novel of its type ever written? Possibly not, although it is the greatest mural of personages both in richness and in its scale that normally and traditionally would be unprecedented in novels of this genre. Which just goes to prove, once and for all, that coruscating truths can be made successfully without all of the excesses and vulgarities being written in.

After Puzo's *The Godfather* and numerous sequels by others, it just seemed to me that the 'Organisation' needed a moderately new lease of life; an enjoyable new lease at that! Whether or not the 'Organisation' deserved or required any such thing is another matter.

This virtually uncut account of Dahlia and Sandra cunningly brings together and then abruptly dispels every kind of prodigal synthesis and popular myth associated with the 'Organisation'. Furthermore, it reduces all of the would-be 'unknowable' into the easily 'lovable' in one funky nihilistic swoop!

Cloudburst is mean, anarchic and shamefully blissful, but first and foremost it is a prime-rate piece of razor-sharp Americana – a huge chocolate box of somewhat overly spiritual intimacy combined with idyllic grandiose ambitions and written by Ricky Dale with almost grandiloquent relentlessness.

At every point in the novel where we might expect to be given visual insights into some messy situation, we are instead given a wrenching tug at our heart strings. It is seldom a novel of this blatant nature comes along and can be enthusiastically enjoyed purely for its superlative narrative value, whilst at the same time as food for quiet humanising thought as well *Cloudburst* pulls it off easily. To discover that Dahlia and Sandra are certainly not villains but rather victims of their own 'peculiarity' comes as something of a relief. In its sentiment, it's a code of accepted behaviour and its attitude towards "a job of work done." This semi-autobiographical account of Dahlia and Sandra may be wholly foreign to our temperament, however please indulge yourselves! It would be the gravest mistake to judge them by our standard of decorum just because they happen to speak the same language as we do ... because they don't!

PRINCIPAL CHARACTERS

This novel is eclectically based upon real events and real perpetrators of those events – although the actuality of certain incentives are sometimes fictionalised. All of the central characters are either loosely based upon real life people, or they feature entirely as palpable aspects of themselves.

Dahlia Carriera
Showgirl/Choreographer
Kim's legally adopted daughter
(mother skedaddled with preacher!)
Raised in Utica USA

Sandra Comanescu
Classical pianist
Kim's legally adopted daughter
(orphaned child)
Raised in Aurora Ontario

'Mom' Provenzano
Superboss of Ontario Organisation
Former opera singer
Ex-wife of 'Big Jim' Colosimo
Resides in Toronto

Kim Comanescu
Former lyric soprano
Half sister of Mom Provenzano
Shares a home with Mom in Toronto

'Blondy' Swanson
Former Organisation soldier
Now Provenzano consigliere

'Uncle' Mike
Problem solver
Younger sibling of RD
Wife Angelica Uizzini (Sicilican Organisation)

Griselda Persico
Bernadette's 'wilful' sister

Bernadette Provenzano
Retired lady of respectable disposition
Second cousin to Mom and Kim

Penny Penniman
Retired Lady of respectable disposition
Second cousin to Mom and Kim

Valeria and Toni Guerriri
Uncle and Aunt who 'ditched' Lillian

Lillian Guerriri
Daughter of above
Adopted by Penny, Dahlia, Sandra and Ricky

Dr Hymia Minsk
'Git-em-up' guy
Octogenarian beau of Penny

'The beautiful' Annabel Lee
Ricky's darlin'!

Lucky (Lemonade) Lucy and
Lola Sapola
Singing and dancing duet
Gay compatriots of Sandra and Dahlia.

PREFACE

WHEN IT ALL boils down, it's about satisfying family values in the end; at least that's the way I construe it! Therefore, to casually describe the spunky escapades of Dahlia and Sandra as merely being a mishmash of 'off the wall' adventures is close to being all, if not somewhat, demeaning. It seems to me that any type of 'description specific' label is verging on being very offensive as well. Theirs is an inherited line of activity that has existed within their respective families for oodles of generations. It is today what it has always been since it was born – a sworn secret society of family members who pursue power and pelf by cultivating the art of killing people and getting away with it.

So why do they do it? For me to take a stab (no pun intended) at giving an overview of Dahlia and Sandra's 'Fuss and Feathers' rationale would be improper to speculate upon. Also it could be potentially risky, inasmuch that I would have broken my word (of honour) to them and put myself in a somewhat invidious predicament!

Enough to say that perhaps that question is impossible to answer in any event. However, from the way I understand it, there has been a buried covenant of traditional ways in the family for getting on three or four hundred years. The politics and people may change, but the historical residue that is passed down remains the same. From runner to runner, like in a relay race, the baton is passed on to the next generation. It's as simple as that!

I came to realise early on that there is a certain 'sinecure' to this line of work. Inasmuch that it involves little or no sweat and grind and you can do quite well out of it – make a killing, so to say! Resourcefulness and some large simoleons, not an arithmetical dilemma. Don't you agree?

It may be that from time to time you develop a kind of dispassion toward Dahlia and Sandra. It may be that you want to change their system, perhaps bring about a nicer resolution (or revolution!). Withal these are bad and harmful acts they are having a hand in and they are such cordial girls. Don't try and make sense of it. With flashbacks, contradiction, ambiguity and even some sleight of hand, you will soon allow yourself to be drawn into their special idiosyncratic netherworld. An unjustifiable world where virtuous and valid reasoning are totally unworkable hogwash and where the so-called concept of immortality is not necessarily 'strictly for the birds' and where life and death are only valid as an over extravagant garden party game.

When I was a small child I remember a saying that we had to sometimes gain sympathy from our Schoolmarm:
"LOOK SEE PIGEON!"

It refers to a person or persons who are easily deceived or duped. Political scientists have been using this clever methodology to maintain the status quo among us morons for decades. So you see, in that regard, all of us already inhabit Dahlia and Sandra's synthetic world of presumption.

It seems to me that there is nothing novel, spectacular, abject or abhorrent regarding some of Dahlia and Sandra's godless ways. Withal each and every great nation in history have, and still do, act as highly successful pedlars of falsehoods. They merely smudge the line a little to make it legal!

Protection, murder, territorial dominance, competition and collaboration between 'gangs', even a hint of a code of honour. In a sense crime is built into our system, isn't it?

Dese, dem and dose situations!

Pulping a grapefruit into Mae Clarke's face, or dragging the poor girl across the room by her hair, wasn't at all naturalistic of the great actor James Cagney. Cagney's role was merely a secondary one. It was, of course, tough guy Tom Powers, the part that Cagney was playing, who gave him entirely the screen dominance to the part. Dahlia summarised it perfectly. Quote – "Once I was in burlesque, now I am in show business, although I guess it's a lot more business than show. The secret of success is just to do whatever dese, dem and dose situations dictate!"

Realistically you require an awful lot of emotional stamina to be totally successful in Dahlia and Sandra's au fait profession. For the most part this line of work has primarily been male dominated and any woman who wishes to smash into this world of men isn't considered as uncompromising enough because of their femininity that gives the female clandestinity. Sandra once very candidly clarified it thus: "I can assure you Ricky that the majority of male assassins are about as discreet as a bull taking a piss in your living room!"

From what I have learned from Dahlia and Sandra is the importance of being unpredictable. For example, you have to ensure that events occur the way in which they seldom do in real life situations. All of the things that are inconceivable to regular folk are the things that will give you your cloak of protection and secrecy. An intrinsic part of you will be scared, this is good, it keeps you alert, but do not resort to panic or you will be on thin ground. The concept of what is too awful to describe will never alter, but it is important to step outside of your comfort zone and to enable you to do this you should use the methods that have proved so successful to others.

What of the so-called morality of it all? This is the 'spitting distance' rundown that Dahlia and Sandra spilled the beans to me about:

'When we are on a job or drawing up a job we never discuss morality or God. We work exclusively in a vacuum. Both Dahlia and I know from the onset precisely what all of our options are. Sometimes those options are tasteful, other times loud and vulgar, but monsters we never become. I would characterize us as maverick spirits who have been endowed with a kind of multitalented creative force!"

"Dahlia and I have learned many ghastly stratagems. We have learned the art of contrivance and how to use illogic and irrationality and put them into effect. Perhaps in some respects that does make us kind of 'monstrous' people, but surely not actual 'monsters'? Mom taught us that there are many physical things that can be seen and touched – like trees and mountains, and they are much more dependable, expressive and honest than most people."

"For us killing folk is almost like an extension of our previous professions. It's a' tour de force' of editing, rehearsing and also some rather outlandish choreography. Not too much rehearsing though because otherwise you can lose that natural spontaneous excitement that comes with each new job. I suppose that each and every job is infused with a kind of wilful eroticism, an impudent childlike imagination, a liberation of sorts – that's what adds to the exhilaration of it all."

"Mom once said that we were both 'queer'. It was a word that freaked me out at the time, although given the choice of not being 'queer' or poking steel pins in my eyes, I'd prefer the steel pins!"

"After our very first execution both Dahlia and I were complexly overwhelmed", Sandra confessed." It was perhaps one of the most deserved yet elegant killings we had ever carried out to date. The respondent was one of the 'High Five' in our organisation, who had apparently 'misbehaved'. I remember thinking afterwards how funny it is how blood stains clothes, yet washes easily off hands. He was a kind of aberrant character in any event. I sometimes thought that when he put his touchy-feely arm around my shoulder at Mass, it was only because it was closer to my throat!"

As for what I know regarding Dahlia and Sandra's relationship – all that I am prepared to let slip is that it is very specific to them only.

Domination, humiliation, masochism; whether these obscurities are implemented in a slight, gradual or a semi-subtle manner, they often seem to cruelly highlight the nature of many relationships these days. However, not so with these two especial, somewhat fearsome entrepreneurs. They are a blood family, they are distinct entities. The sad thing is by the time I get to really know them, they may be gone.

Confusion (from *A Suite of Mirrors*)
Is my heart
Your heart?
Who is mirroring my thoughts?
Who lends me this
Unrooted passion?
[…]

Federico Garcia Lorca

PART 1

Triumvirate

Love is: more
than being warm in bed
and more
than an individual seeking an accomplice
and much more
than just wanting to share

Resume One (Sandra)

In just a little while from now I'm going to have a shot at recounting to you the precise day when, in Sandra Comanescu's topsy-turvy reasoning, she began to become totally aware of her sexuality and its unconscious choice.

She had thought of love and sex as a mystery, especially the beginning, the moment of falling in love. One of her hush-hush pastimes was trying to understand the so-called dynamics of her playfellows. For example: What does she see in him? Why does she stay with him? Will it last? Why do they quarrel all the time? Why does he never show her affection? She puzzled and puzzled to little avail, indeed she found it mountainously impossible to come to terms with her own every day inclinations, let alone anyone else's! The 'discombobulated' gravitations she had, to which her Priest had cautioned her about, were what bothered her the most and yet in just a little while from now she would learn life's great esoteric secret, that everyone is undiscovered and often alone, until someone out there says ... hello!

Today was going to be the precise day when Sandra Comanescu would learn about 'exceptions to the rule' and, furthermore, she would learn that these exceptions are so powerful and plentiful that they ride out there on the very air that we breathe. All you've got to do is to reach out quickly and snatch one before it has time to disappear. That's all! To a certain extent it's really quite as simplistic as that, or otherwise there wouldn't be any point or reason for being a mere 19 years of age, would there?

Empty is: more
than a snowy morning
(in 1973)

Folks riding trains are often overly nice to you. Something of an example would be the offer of a magazine or some chocolate covered peanuts or, if you are really fortuitous, they may wish to tell you all the unpleasant details (you don't really want to know) about their recent operations!

Sandra was a respectful listener and had she been journeying homeward she probably would have enjoyed all of that unimportant chit-chat and listened intently with both ears. However, she was journeying far away from home for another forty-eight week tour. Already she felt miles and worlds away from anything that was or is. She felt detached from the vast carriage and its passengers and wondered what words of sensibility or source of comfort could ever assure her that in another week she would be ready for all of that stage mithering again.

Empty and stone-faced she gazed disconnectedly through the frosted Triplex glass and out across the vast divide of rheumy locomotive rails watching the almost ritual quiet saddened snow fall in wild and dizzy patterns. Her eyes cold and empty, like the eyes you see of animals in cages when all of everything has been taken away from them and only an unconscious desire for their own death remains.

Seemingly undecided the Pullman cars and timber laden wagons hobbled steadfastly onto their eventual rails, the tracks that would seamlessly transit Sandra all the way to Penn, NY was well-nigh a day's journey away, yet already Sandra's longing for home was becoming embarrassingly restless. How will it be when the tour kicks-off proper?

Just yesterday she had sat in the makeup chair in Studio 11 wondering why she was there. I too wondered why, withal she has a perfectly proportioned face, beautiful high cheekbones and looks striking even without makeup and, for heaven's sake, she is a pianist, not a movie star. Albeit she is Canada's greatest pianistic talent of recent years, even though she was only just becoming known, there were nevertheless several eyebrow rousing passengers on the train to Penn. It seemed conspicuous that they thought they knew who Sandra was, but on the other hand were a little too undecided to pose the question "Aren't you … ?" She had seen it happen before and for that reason she just kept her eyes in her lap. Sensible girl!

I take the view that Sandra's recent disintegration of her own differences between popularity and normalcy is similar to a Hershey bar that tastes good at the time but it kills dinner later on. It seems to me that Sandra's appetite is of late to the point where even memory of popularity is not a feast for her any longer ... if indeed it ever was so! The Locomotor tagged along through trees and ridges, she had no complaints any longer, she knew the battle was hopeless for her.

Very soon the coniferous evergreens that swept cosyingly across the seemingly infinite landscape were becoming like thinly scattered brooms. Repetitive residences of lath board lumber and deep brownish red brick buildings were slowly taking their place. Bedazzling rain and fog had more than interrupted the snow's weary ability to take over and even the air was feeling different as the city neared.

The city scape intruded gradually but somewhat beyond the expected or acceptable limits she had envisaged. It grew and beckoned, as cities do, with each onward motion of the train. She promised herself to be at ease, unworried, relaxed and confident but all of those unqualified promises were just emoting to little pieces before her.

Far off in Montreal, whilst the purse prize makers were rapaciously congratulating their astute arses, their uninterchangeable Cinderella was dialectically dying.

Sandra had long given up on her fractious search for her so-called Prince Charming. He really never was or, for that matter, never could be. Indeed, when the chips were finally down, it was she who was undecided as to whether she wanted a Prince Charming in any event!

What troubled me at the time was that there wasn't a wrong side or a right side to the 'Sandra' equation at all and that the correct answer was just about to explode in optimism, implode in its pessimism and quite honestly for Sandra it would never remain bland and indifferent ever again.

Resume Two (Dahlia)

Born in Brooklyn and raised in a shuffle of dreary upstate towns, was it any wonder that Dahlia soon got the hang of using her tears like poison darts? Looking back to half-remembered yesterdays when some felonious reward consisted of chocolate bars and nickel bubble gum, nowadays only the value of the contribution had changed and still she had never forgotten how to cry!

'Don't blacken up your eyes, your tears are messing my pillow'! Dahlia's men seemed either incapable or incompetent to provide any kind of enthusiasm that survived too long – a rigorous moment to moment was par for the course! She never met a man yet who wasn't capable of making small distances even smaller once the needing was over.

When it was time to go, Dahlia would always go softly, so as not to wake up the neighbour's dog or some such. Dahlia was really good at exits! She knew the score and exactly which part of her mind it should be kept in. She also knew how to cross a darkened room naked and without a flashlight – she knew too how to cross herself in the event the intensity of her demons was just too great!

Dahlia had dropped her moon into the shimmery cold pool many times in the past and for that reason she was more than adapt at recovering it again. She had long past began to be the gilly flower of any number of men. She had become devoid of all of those 'too soon' feelings of astonishment and mind-blowing 'remarkability'. In all actuality men had become just a 'sure thing' to Dahlia, as perhaps she was to them.

Despite all that, this cowgirl was still youthful and crackbrained enough to fold her legs around and hold fast to any inappropriately named 'bronc' that destiny had decidedly chosen to hurl her way. Having said all that, she wouldn't have any likelihood of continually eating dust for him or indeed any nondescript stranger, either singular or plural!

Initiation

Fates most distinctive component!

WHEN SISTER DAHLIA boarded the 3.10 to Penn Station her timing was precisely on the button, just as Mom and Kim had predicted it would be. Mom didn't want her cherished Dahlia loitering around the station more than was necessary. It was rumoured that certain folk in Utica were poisonously divided and uncharitable toward Mulatto peoples, in fact anyone of a coloured disposition! It troubled Mom a lot that there are those who demand their kind of freedom bad enough to take away their neighbours' in the process. Here on the far side of time it was important that Mom grasped matters from a business woman's standpoint. "We must keep a good sense of perspective about what we've done in the past and what we aim to achieve in the future" she often dryly remarked.

Informally Mom was affectionately known as 'Padrino', especially by the many old stagers. In a more literal sense she was 'Superboss' who it was whispered was gifted enough to seek out 'soon to be targets' from her so-called psychic readings. However, it seems to me that she didn't often read a predicted event that wasn't entirely predetermined in the first place!

Some years ago, in an unusually unorthodox disclosure, Mom let be known to me her intimate reflective on matters of business and such. Quote: "Amid all of the chaos of new garbage we quietly become very adept at hate, good enough in any event to call ourselves true professionals!"

"Jesus died for somebody's sins, but not mine"
Patti Smith

It's comparatively unchallenging to assume that, equipped with a xerographic copy of a person, you should be able to identify them immediately. However, the process of recognising and being recognised in reciprocal unison is perhaps not as simplistic as you would imagine it to be, particularly when the xerographic copy is at least a dozen years old! Someone should have told them that Mom had a warped sense of humour. She didn't want Dahlia and Sandra's get-together to be too uncomplicated!

Despite Mom's jest, Dahlia and Sandra's eyes met immediately Dahlia entered the compartment, no matter how hesitatedly they tried to play it cool, the bond was forged.

By the time the train grinded to a halt at Poughkeepsie they had sung a succession of rock ballads and most of 'Me and Bobby McGee'. Their predilections were outside of themselves and enshrouded in one another. "You are the same someone as I am" Dahlia declared excitedly. Unashamedly Sandra responded over and over, ditto, ditto, ditto.

Cloudburst

"Don' cha understand? Music is just about feelin'
things and havin' a good time!"

Janis Joplin, 1968

Triumvirate

An elucidation

IF YOU DECIDE that you do want to become an active participant within the Organisation there are various rules that must be observed with regard to 'dialogue' and 'introductions'. That is, of course, unless you have been 'hot-rodded' into the Organisation by family interconnections etc such as Dahlia and Sandra would have been. This unusual dialogue skirts around being somewhat unclear and undecided and yet it unmistakably confirms a very simple and very important line of reasoning. So much so that even its practitioners are often unaware of each other's objectives. For example 'carefully considered' or 'purposefully wilful' can have letter for letter the same connotations which all goes to prove that 'death' per se is not such a fearsome character once it has been thoroughly understood.

Withal, even a poem is not meant to be understood by everyone and regrettably an ample amount of British poetry does actually (though painlessly) put you to sleep. Try it!

PART 2

Cherchez La Femme

DAHLIA CARRIERA WAS nothing if not a star. Why, no one could have been blessed with more varied acting abilities than Dahlia possessed in her pinky finger alone, or could have sung and danced any better, have been more statuesquely beautiful or more sweetly pretty or unashamedly sexy.

Dahlia Carriera was four-square determined to claw, nail and talon, out and away from backwoods USA and, with that dispassionate objective in mind, she worked duplicitously tirelessly to achieve it. Morning, noon and night conscientiously modelling and remodelling herself until she was absolutely certain that she had built a personality that she was entirely comfortable with and confident in.

Every little shop girl has at some time stretched her wandering imagination to become the next singing star or movie queen, or some such. Dahlia, on the other hand, was not into a relationship of any type with pure fantasy. She unquestionably knew that everything was there for the taking and she wanted totally everything and nothing less would be adequate for her.

Dahlia was far too intellectual to want a husband. Although she had lived with other women and men from time to time, not necessarily in the way it implies, nonetheless she had never considered that there may be some sort of veiled over benefit in having a husband. However, fortune have it, there always was an acceptable supplementary of over-energetic spouses searching for some sprightly dalliances.

Dahlia adored Christmas, not that she presumed it would bring her some dewy-eyed nostalgia of Christmas' past, but more likely that it would bring her some blithe jerk who was exercising his Christmas gratuity. So it was on the first Saturday evening in December, before the sound of sleigh bells from the Buffalo carnival had faded away, Dahlia and Dexter Albright (of the Delaware Dish Company) were crammed with food and wine and cosseting quid pro quo!

Appropriately, according to Dahlia's philosoph, life and living it successfully is like some of the greatest works of art – nice to look at, but fundamentally abstract! Someone had once defined her as a 'terminal protestant' because of her ethic values. The comparison for me was pretty clear when she told me that for her "life was a semi-rich comedy with several hundred or so different integrated interpretations and ideological guises in it!"

Dahlia is, and for me always will be, an exceptionally pretty young provocateur who is so infuriatingly lascivious in cuckolding geriatric Sugar Daddies (who really do enjoy lavishing gifts) it's not hardly any sort of twisted reality in an imaginary world that they themselves have both created … is it??

In any event, dear Dahlia only viewed reality as a constraint of sorts and therefore she contrived to stay away from its claws as much as promiscuousness would allow: getting too close to the 'reality' of her so-called quarry would be boringly obscene to her.

Pretty soon it would be progressively that time again to renew herself. That was indeed the true genius of Dahlia Carriera. Always the perfect actress who never forgot her lines, or indeed his partialities. When the red curtain of his overindulgence finally falls it will only leave a secret that she is able to lose, but regain a thousand times over at her own discretion.

PART 3

Between Mirrors

JUST BEFORE SHE opened the cabin door she paused and looked up at the heavy overloaded sky. There's going to be a mighty snow storm she thought and hurried inside to warmth.

Mom had already started supper and had got going an energetic cracking fire in the fireplace. The fireplace had been a needless extravagance to install with much labour required – and withal they had oil fire heating installed years ago, however, Sandra loved to watch the fire as she ate and for that matter, so did Mom. Never mind that they're dirty and old-fashioned, or the chimney doesn't draw and fills the cabin with smoke, or that it makes you squawk when a spark hits you. Just you gaze into a roaring fire, there are so many entrancing and unshared secrets. I guess that's the mere beauty of having a fireplace.

By now the wind was howling like a bitch on heat. Sandra stood up and pulled the curtain back slightly and pressed her face against the glass, making blinders with her hands on her forehead "Blowing up a real blizzard Mom." "Been lookin' like it since three o'clock this afternoon" Mom casually replied. Sandra gazed at Mom and smiled, her eyes were very nearly overflowing with love for her.

After supper they drank cocoa and Mom recounted

several chipper anecdotes regarding some of her dead relatives' capers and then they radiantly went to bed. Mom's stories were always a stimulant for sleep. Almost unconsciously Sandra's mind registered that the wind was fiercely driving icy pellets of snow against her bedroom window glass. She wrapped the woollen blanket tightly around her body and drifted contentedly and gladly into Mom's urban myths and beyond.

*

Dahlia always lit up her darkness. Sandra knew that Dahlia loved her even though she was still a virgin. In any event Sandra didn't honestly know what virginity meant. She thought that being a virgin meant being good like the Virgin Mary. In her adolescent mind, virginity stood for goodness, humility, gentleness and selflessness. She didn't think that she could come even close enough to those sentiments and so perhaps she wasn't a virgin after all because she could never be that good! At seventeen she didn't have the slightest idea what exactly the sex act was all about. Meanwhile she did know her sex was there even if she didn't know where the drive was!

Without a clue what was really happening to her, she confused healthy normality with promiscuity and depravity. Once, at a little birthday party, someone asked her what her star sign was. Virgo the Virgin she replied and added "I don't look like one, do I?" At fourteen or fifteen years old she still didn't understand why the guests were squirming in their chairs and snickering at her, but for all her not knowing, she knew (and never forgot) that everyone's laughter was something she didn't want to know right then or again. Odd though it may seem, although Sandra did not know what virginity meant, in her diary she wrote down all the things that her sexual 'ignorance' got her into, like never really catching the double entendre art of that sheer ignorance!

The way it was for Sandra was that she loved Kim and Mom so dearly. Once she decided who to trust she followed their lead – she listened and she learned. She remembered telling Kim about a girl she was in love with. Unfortunately the girl liked somebody else. Kim listened, thought about it and then said plainly "You better take care of your piano studies Sweetipie because if they fail as well, you'll be twice as unhappy as you are now"!

Kim and Mom believed in the power of having a certain simplicity in life whether it had to do with work or relationships. Mom used to say "Boil it all down to what counts the most Sweetipie. What is the essence of what you are trying to do, what is the most important thing? Remember that things get complicated when you are trying to address too many issues." Perhaps Kim and Mom were right, because without the 'sex' issue to complicate her life, Sandra emerged as a powerful adult person. Strong-willed and sure of what she wanted she was, as some liked to describe her, a steel hand in a velvet glove … and a gentle heart who truly deserved a truly magical human being. She didn't need a second opinion for that!

PART 4

'Amour Propre'

DAHLIA TIPTOED ACROSS the room to the small divan bed where Sandra was resting. She carefully positioned herself on the flaky eiderdown and, although the bed hardly sank at all with her meaningless weight, Sandra was awake in a jiffy. Sandra was always two steps ahead of everyone; it was just her nature to be that way and she kind of suspected what Dahlia was finding so hard to bring up. Indeed, in matters of the heart, Sandra could unmask St Valentine himself!

She looked at Dahlia's criss-cross over highlighted eyebrows and smiled with fondness "explicitly no! dear Dahlia, there isn't a boy" and then feeling that Dahlia still needed some reassurance she cut in and added "not then, not now, not anymore." She empathised so much because of Dahlia's fear of rejection. She topped-off the whole confusion by smacking a funky kiss on Dahlia's face just above her eyebrows!

With a snicker that was not less that cheekily happy, Dahlia nuzzled up to Sandra closely "Oh, I needed that, I needed you, I did, I do!" Dahlia had just attempted to say what should always be said and finished in a million lifetimes by lovers of the heart. However, it only took but one look from Sandra to say it right back to her.

On that teensy New York island, and in their minuscule New York apartment, they had both discovered a palatial mountainside, a sumptuous rich fabric of sign-posts and neon signs directing and inspiriting them and giving them both the answers, changes and announcing coming miracles true, sure and soon.

Sandra and Dahlia lay together like nursling plants; leggy and like-minded to aspire and rejoice heights of resolute dispensation.

They'd been waiting all this time, hoping and thinking that the world was waiting just beyond their world for them and now it wouldn't matter anymore. Soundlessly, happy and satisfied, that something they were waiting for was ready and they were ready to make it their own.

Just listening to the taxicabs blowing their horns through the open window and into their bedroom was heaven. Just hearing the pigeons cooing voices on the stoop in the seconds of quiet between the honking was ecstasy. Just feeling the stickiness of skin against skin was literally all and everything, because tomorrow they could do it all again – that was the certainty of their love.

PART 5

Reminiscence

IT WAS A drizzly wet Saturday. Warm steady drizzle that seemed to turn the whole city grey. For their part Dahlia and Sandra truly enjoyed a leisurely stroll through Central Park in the rain. It was a privacy thing – holding hands and kissing. Something they felt was restricted to do on a populously sunny day. There was the occasional jogger of course, but they were pretty much focussed on their passion, not to be waylaid by girls kissing and such. However, when this big guy started running toward them they both grabbed at each other. They were quick to realise he was a jogger, not a mugger, and almost simultaneously they turned red with embarrassment. Dahlia took the tiny Star of David from around her neck and kissed it whilst Sandra, not being a Jeremiah, just thanked her elusive lucky stars instead.

Sandra looked deep into Dahlia's eyes, there was something of herself in them. "Do you want a High School Boy or me to protect you"? she said. "Blah! Blah! Blah!" Dahlia replied. "I want tarts and tea when we get home and then I'll let you know." The rain was so insuperable to ruin and they were so indebted to it.

Men have so much to learn about rain Sandra suddenly interceded into Dahlia's sexual euphemistic obscurities. "Once I kissed a boy – a boy named Michael

– in the seventh grade. He wore braces that made him lisp. Whenever he was around me he was always nervous and fumbling, offering to carry my books and buy me sodas and such. I did sort of like him and one day I just up and kissed him. I had never kissed anyone on the lips before. We just sat there in the park with our lips pressed together until Michael pulled away. After that he purposely avoided me. It was as though he grew scared of me suddenly." Me; I just wondered if I'd ever kiss someone again?

Dahlia's eyes grew dark and serious. It was Yom Kippur and I sat at the top of the stairs listening to a white-haired loser telling me about his love for all mankind and coaxing me toward the lump in his swimming trunks. "Come on!" he said and took my hand to lead me. I felt his grip through my whole arm for days afterward.

Years after, sitting at the top of those stairs I still shivered as uncontrollably as I had done during that night.

'Assignations' were obliged to happen in those days. Chastity was only considered chastity if it was met by obedience. He was a respected 'nuncio' in the Roman Catholic Church and so a fiction was maintained that he was a special friend – a strictest secret, special friend. Not one Sister of Mercy had refused to collude. They had even planted a hemlock hedge between the novices two houses and the convent to 'protect the girls privacy' from curious eyes.

Dahlia's eyes were wet, but not with tears running down her cheek. Her tears were permeable, spongy, they had been absorbed – they had abided and patiently endured. Sandra brought her a glass of rich sherry, there was something about their lives together, their attachment was deep yet not yet quite fathomed by mere mortals.

"The soul selects her own society
Then – shuts the door –
To her divine majority
Present no more"

Emily Dickinson

*

Dahlia gazed long and lovingly at Sandra "You know in those days I could not sleep at night for thinking that somehow God would decide to make me immortal" – immortality was my apotheosis of absolute horror.

"We were like aspiring nineteenth century women Sandra, struggling to do their duty to impress the Illuminati in their pantheons of power." That's what we were like Sandra.

Dahlia had long had her own presentiment of a special fate, maybe some stardom of her own yet, like Kim, she wanted to be seen to emerge from her array of talents. She longed to be recognised as 'herself' first and foremost. She was heading toward that realisation to find the larger truth when she and Kim first met and now she was only eager to share Sandra's love for the unpretentious aspects of life. The misty falls in winter, the red maples in autumn and the innumerable voice of the gossip crickets and a heady summer's evening.

Sandra had once confided in her that she hoped to have crickets chirping around her grave one day. Now

Dahlia was convinced that she wanted the same! It always seemed to me that modest domesticity was Kim's cover for her soul's immensity. If we turn our eyes away from her tame visible life, if we breakthrough her somewhat clockwork routines, we come across an amazing person who may or may not, at her own peril, engage in a life of love and a love of life that will imprint itself upon all so-called socially acceptable behaviour.

Though tough, both Sandra and Dahlia were also so delicate beyond expression. Not even Henry James in his portrait of a Lady could give a realistic account of Isabel Archer – at least one that won't make your snore and so I would be struggling in immensity to provide an explanation of why real life can, in its way, be much more extraordinary than fictional lives.

"For what is each instant but a gun, harmless
because 'unloaded', but that touched 'goes off'?"
Emily Dickinson

With the exception of Shakespeare, both Dahlia and Sandra have given me more to write about than anyone I can name!

'Blackfriars' or Black Friars has a Masonic symbolism

In the beginning Eve slopped around laboriously. Cain tried to find the right channel so as he could listen to pop music and Abel catnapped most of the day. Adam, fully aware of his actions, set out toward Heaven. I guess it's called a continuous action – whilst everybody is doing absolutely nothing, yet at the same time they are also all looking for 'approval'.

In 1982 Carlos Marcello awoke one morning feeling that he needed 'approval'. He was getting on in years and as a God-fearing Catholic he wanted restitution and retribution (he died in 1993). He had never met Dahlia Carriera, but he had met nuncio of the Catholic Church Robert Calvi – then known as 'God's Banker'. After The Banco Ambrosiano collapsed due to millions of dollars missing from its books, the Vatican was strongly implicated and so was 'God's Banker'. Calvi was later found hanging from Blackfriars Bridge in London, England. The day before his body was found his private secretary, Graziella Corrocher, jumped to her death from a fifth floor window at the Banco Ambrosiano.

It would appear that 'God's Banker' may have been 'suicided' because the Vatican had mentioned to Messr Carlos Marcello that Calvi was 'unreliable' – and then turned a blind eye.

It seems to me that the disrespectful and 'unregulated' word *Mafia* has become a fabrication of blame. However, perhaps a secret justice society *does* exist – a society that is more concerned with so-called power and influence than with money per se – something that it seems to me to be quite courageous!

Some years ago I heard a story about a former priest who became a sort of vigilante against crime. It was rumoured that he often administered the last rites to some of his own victims, at least from time to time!

I guess that one way or another God pays debts without money and I like to imagine that Calvi got his just desserts for his wrongful dalliance with young girls and that the misappropriation of Vatican cash was, well coincidental?

Although Dahlia and Sandra were hardly the Bronte sisters, they did occasionally put pen to paper, particularly detailed descriptions of places they had visited together. It took a lot of persuasion, several months in fact, before they finally and almost dutifully allowed me access to their notes on their visit to Europe. Sandra had been a might apprehensive about the trip at first – she was fundamentally a small town girl and, although she had stretched her horizons to Manhattan, at least it was on the same continent!

Dahlia however convinced her about how well she would look after her, and that this would be an exciting and impressive adventure. The fact that Dahlia spoke fluent French finally made the argument and they reserved a cabin on the SS America – so finally – at last – they were on their way.

They shared their cabin with two other girls; one was a Swiss girl who spent every night putting her Swiss imprints on the Purser's sheets! The other 'girl' sharing their cabin was 99 year old Miss Stanyon. Sandra recalled how Miss Stanyon had frightened her enough with her clothes on, but one night when she turned the lights on at about

3am she was horrified to see Miss Stanyon's bony, naked body heading to the bathroom. On the second day out they met two Ali Khan type guys from Lebanon who were like flirtatious puppies. Dahlia finally managed to dissuade them by straight from the shoulder mentioning hers and Sandra's dykey partiality. Dahlia said "those guys have deeper motives". Sandra was intrigued by Dahlia's references and in the quirkiness of the sex lives of Near Easterners!

When the ship finally arrived at Le Havre six days later all Sandra seemed preoccupied with was feeding the pigeons in Saint Roch Square Park. Dahlia, on the other hand, was more ambitious. She wanted to climb that mountain in the Pyrenees where you can sit in France and gaze at Spain.

That's the way they were Dahlia and Sandra; like gypsy vagabonds the pair of them. Kind of like beautiful cats – cats, wrestling amid the chaos of life's garbage, never caring about supercilious distinctions, just two inverse quantities in love with each other and their objectives!

PART 6

Favara Brotherhood

THE CRUMBLING OLD guard of the Sicily Organisation had become somewhat out of touch with the fast-paced modern world of late. However, it was still vicious enough to do some unequivocal second to none damage when absolutely necessary. My heart will always belong to a select abundance of those self-appointed seniors and the chivalrous demeanour of their soldiers. Sometimes I have such wonderful thoughts about their so-called 'sensibilities', however, it's impossible to 'pass on' to you what they are because I know for sure that no one can really understand them but me. For example, if you don't like a certain story it is not the story that is to blame it is probably because you and I cannot identify with it – you cannot find yourself in it! A certain episode or character, sometimes perhaps a sentence that gives me the words I want to explain it to you. When it all boils down the fault is mine – the fault is the something I always knew but never had the words to explain it. In any event it seems to me that every reader finds their own story between the pages of a book, but whether or not the story is a great story and exactly why it is such, I am tempted to say you should find out for yourself. Perhaps it's like the adventure story Treasure Island inasmuch that we are all armed with a map showing the location of the buried treasure, but only

Squire Trelawney has the acumen and the perseverance to achieve the task.

It was the inflexible attitude of those old guard guys that I admired the most and I am reminded of their scattergun philosophies over again. Some evenings I remember them as I walk home from work, usually around the part where I am half way home, I just want to kneel down and kiss the asphalt and thank God for more than my daily bread. You see, to be told that you can "kill" anyone can have a profound effect on a young guy and I didn't really want to know about Vatican history and how they think that they are telling the truth, even when they are lying. Even though many years have passed and those old guys have probably long passed on by now, the echoes still live on in my head. I really couldn't write without them. Although (it may sound odd – and probably is) how I use them is strictly my own secret. It seems to me, in an incredulously indelible way, that nobody can be trusted and everybody lies all of the time and so please do not sell me hope when there ain't any! I learned a long time ago, and saw the proof, that you can go far with a Ricky Dale smile, but you can go a lot further with a smile and a gun!

By his desk Ibsen kept a tray of little animals – dogs and cats, wooden bears, a rabbit playing a fiddle and so on. He once said "I never write a single line of my plays without that tray and its occupants in front of me on the table." They obviously symbolized the encapsulation of his thoughts and perhaps summation of mine too! Just before his death Ibsen wrote: "We all sail with a corpse in the cargo." I have mulled over his idea that we are all dominated by the past and indeed tend to agree that this is probably a popular viewpoint.

However, it is the minority that is always right on so many random occasions. That is to say the minority that is leading a specific route toward the same point at which the majority has not yet arrived; in perhaps ten years time the majority will probably come round to the point of view that the minority has! However, during those ten years the minority will not have been standing still and once again they will be at least ten years ahead of the majority. This is not necessarily my thought on the matter, it is one of Sandra's more profound whimsies. She asked me to put it into the book to help get it out of her system!

So to sum up this somewhat laborious chapter, perhaps it is only the best stories that are able to inspire us. Stories that personify the weaknesses and the virtues, the feelings and the thoughts that we all share. More than often the story itself and its characters and situation may even in some respect be a parchment of our own lives and so, like good friends, they follow us on our journey and with each beat of our heart we are reminded of them again and again.

Although I cannot 'pass on' to you my thoughts I promise that, just as windmills turn, you also will turn, not with the wind, but slowly and imperceptibly away from what is called normality. These following pages will be quite a journey and you won't come back the way you started, if you are as lucky as I know you will be!

PART 7

The Voices

BLINKING LIKE AN owl and still thick throated Dahlia awakened with a jump startling both herself and Sandra. "Oh my!" she said drenched in perspiration; "I've been nightmaring again." Sandra tangled herself around the distressed Dahlia and kicked the hot chequered bed cover onto the floor. "It's OK" she reassuringly responded "it's still last night – I still love you."

Some things demand a finding out about and some loose strings need tying or perhaps untying. Sometimes an empty space needs walking through, if only to prove it ever existed! Dahlia had always portrayed herself as the self-assured assertive incalculable individual.

Sandra needed to know where Dahlia's memories went when alone at night and eternity sneaks tenaciously by. She needed to know that it wasn't merely her thighs that speak Dahlia's name and that Sandra truly had that resolve and that responsibility to help and she knew it.

Sometimes it's hard to speculate on what the cluttered mind saves beyond too many winters, and sometimes we don't really need to look back that far. The sun would seldom catch Sandra lying in bed late, but she would lie there with Dahlia until Dahlia could find sanity again and share the one face of herself that she held back on for years.

Dahlia's account

Dahlia crinkled her nose in distaste: "I was a wayward girl when I was 10 or 11. I used to let boys look up my dress for a dime. Although I never had any sex with a random guy, I kind of crazily hero-worshipped the girls who worked the street. My mom was a saloon singer in an unsalubrious district and I would go along with her most evenings in preference to being left all alone. I studied the street girls and I learned their mannerisms. The way they talked out of the sides of their mouths with a cigarette dangling from a corner. I acquired their speech inflections. I watched how they drank their liquor and picked up guys. I just completely immersed myself, even mimicking the cheapness of their swagger."

"Then one day, sandwiched between my mom and the street girls, there was a preacher and the PTA who decided that my summertime was done and I wound up in a correctional establishment, namely the 'Ontario School of Industry' which was a reform school without walls."

"For a while I was the youngest girl there and being small and coloured and not from 'Canadiana' made me the logical and easy inmate to blame. Punishment was delegated to a so-called 'Commissary' who was a senior member of a committee run by the older girls. Names were drawn from a hat and, depending upon which older girl was finally nominated, dictated your final punishment. Some girls enjoyed dishing out severe punishment, other girls let you off lightly. For example, a dozen cane lashes were normal, although sometimes restriction, like being locked in a cupboard for several days or not going into town to the movies for a month or two (the Saturday treat). The 'victims' had no way of knowing they had been accused of something that day. Indeed, whether the accusation was true or false, did not really matter because often it was all a vicious plan that the older girls had concocted themselves."

Sandra held her tight. "Is it fair that you sleep through eternity so troubled – while I am left alive and awake to trouble over why you sleep this way?" Dahlia, poised with calmness and confidence replied "You don't have to touch me to be touching me, nor feel my body to be feeling my body, yet sometimes touching you makes me feel I am so insufficient, which I am!"

PART 8

Enigmatic Food For Thought

HE WAS A mime artist until he began gazing at himself and began losing all perspective. It was as though he was devouring all of his own physiognomy. Even his wrinkled palms were becoming humid and mummified in an unprecedented, unprejudiced and unpremeditated gesture of sheer anxiety and cool detachment he vanished. Not like dinosaurs vanish, but wholly and absolutely and despairingly!

Sometimes when a favour is asked there is no logic, and why must there be any type of logic in any event? Already scientists maintain the foetus has the ability to dream and so even before entering this world we are expecting the 'favour' and completely eager for absolutely whatever action is necessary!

Allie 'tick tock' Tannenbaum is probably one of my favourite personalities in the annals of Jewish gangsters. Some claim that Tannenbaum disappeared and spent the rest of his life as a hat salesman in Atlanta before he went missing off the Florida coast in 1976 – a 'plausible' absence??

PART 9

Cum Granulo Salis

"I hope your rambles have been sweet and your
reveries spacious"

Emily Dickinson

"NINETY-NINE DEGREES IN the shade, and there aint no
shade." Dahlia fanned herself with her new white straw
hat and sipped genteelly upon Sandra's summertime
concoction of gin and iced grapefruit juice. The sky was
as bright blue as a sailor's tunic, the sun was enormously
hurtful and not a wisp of cloud was to be seen.

Sandra lowered herself into the long chair under the
impasto tree. It was the kind of chair that Dahlia would
call a "chaise lounge". Sandra ruminated over the French
meaning 'chaise' was French for chair and surmised that
it certainly was a chair for 'lounging'.

They had a comfortable little room at the San Antonio
Hotel. Sandra was particularly fond of the room service
menu which included her favourite homemade bran
muffins. Dahlia on the other hand was partial to the
tortilla soup. Perched up there on their hotel veranda it
was difficult to imagine a hotel with such an inappropri-
ate name; withal this was Rome and the Colosseum was
resting close by.

"Sing to me Dahlia" Sandra implored.

"Only if you'll give up eating dairy products" Dahlia loquaciously replied and reinforced it with "dairy products produce phlegm while singing!"

Carl Robert Belew was an American songwriter – they dated for a while during the 1970s. This is one of his:

I'm looking for that lonely street
I've got a sad, sad tale to tell
I need a place to go and weep
Where's this place called Lonely Street?
A place where there's just loneliness
Where dim lights bring forgetfulness
Where broken dreams and memories meet
Where's this place called Lonely Street?
Perhaps upon that lonely street
There's someone such as I
Who came to bury broken dreams
And watch an old love die.
If I could find that lonely street
Where dim lights bring forgetfulness
Where broken dreams and memories meet
Where's that place called Lonely Street?

"That love is all there is, is all we know of love"
Emily Dickinson

PART 10

A Curious Journey

WHY TAKE A journey to a far-off foreign country in spite of its exotic nature unless of course you have a liking toward 'foreigners', or perhaps that the concept of foreignness has always somewhat eluded you and you wish therefore to be 'educated'? Why indeed, when right here on your own doorstep out in the breezy, flowery, grand old woods you can hear the wind gossiping with the leaves and the squirrels capering over you and around you and the tiny birds filling the tranquil solitude with music?

Unless it's to keep a note of someone's grave to make certain it's in good condition, that the fences and head-stones are kept painted or whitewashed and are replaced by new ones as soon as they begin to look rusty or decayed and that the walkways are clean and smooth and gravelled.

It seems to me that the Organisation preferred a euphemistic approach to death. I guess that when referring to something or someone unpleasant or conceivably embarrassing, less direct sentences are an excellent alternative!

Dahlia and Sandra were by all accounts (so I'm told!) better by far than the proverbial rattlesnake, inasmuch that they didn't produce a 'rattling sound' or, in other words, they didn't disturb the 'status quo'!

Dahlia and Sandra were the most exemplary 'expressive' pall bearing mourners and occupied a prominent place at whichever or whatever sermon or soon-to-be (prospective!) casual elimination. Right down to the last sentence of the prayer they would guarantee the dead person's soul ascended and invariably respond with a loud "AMEN!".

The plumed hearse, the dirge-breathing brass band, the closed business, the flags drooping at half-mast, the procession of secret societies – all of that degree of grandeur was taken care of by 'others'. Dahlia and Sandra's involvement was the most basic level of activity – at grassroots level you might say with not so much as a 'ciao'!

First the binoculars, then the rifle to the eye and everything else follows the normal course of events! "Never gander" Sandra said; "Just move on!"

PART 11

'The Castigation'

IT WAS STILL fairly early in the morning and small business guys were opening up their joints for the day. No one was about to take any notice of two young Yanks as they made their way along Blackfriars Road to the Southbank Centre. There was a garden that Sandra adored there, an actual authentic garden right in the centre of London, filled with wild flowers, vegetable patches … and a bar!

A big, six foot two guy with straw coloured hair and a matching moustache (who they had christened 'Blondy' Swanson) met them at the entrance. "Did you chastise the scoundrel?" he smiled. *"Sh-h-h"* replied Sandra, "I seem to remember we did."

'Blondy' Swanson was a well respected and totally irreligious boss! Yet later that year it was reported this His Holiness Pope John Paul II found time in the Vatican to clasp Swanson's hands fervently between his own which could only be described as an embrace. The Holy Father's attention was always on the ball – justifiably so!

PART 12

'OMERTA'

Secret Societies and so-called Secret Organisations have long since time immemorial been all-powerful. Regardless of by which political administration, a state, or community is ruled, neither liberalism nor unification will in all honesty enhance or improve the ordinary Joe's lot. However, these surreptitious 'camorra' can. They are a constantly expanding group of go-getting entrepreneurs who endeavour to equally distribute the earnings of all, and keep up a fond intercourse with inappropriately named outcasts and take under their wing alleged malefactors.

For this they place great importance upon silence and non-co-operation with outside authorities, together with a non-interference in the internal matters of its groups.

The Provenzano 'offsprings' paid little attention to the goings on in the teeming cities, however, within the 'camorra' they were very much especial insiders and from time to time they demonstrated their appreciation with relish!

PART 13

'Tick, Tock, Tick'

IN HABERSHAM COUNTY, at the gateway to the North Georgia Mountains, lies the small picturesque town of Cornelia, just 261 miles from Tallahasse and the Florida coast. There were quite a few 'snowbirds' nestling in the Florida sun, that long harsh Manhattan winter of 1975.

Sandra always seemed to have an apron on of late. Indeed, she resembled a little house mother, cooking away. Cooking and tasting the garlicky sauce and the macaroni tubes. She could be so different in the kitchen, perhaps not unlike a Canadian Stepford temperament, that was Sandra.

Outgoing dreamer Dahlia sat pensively upon the worn Chesterfield pre-occupied in her deep thought. "So what's your story De? What are you thinking about?" Sandra enquired. "I was just recalling" she replied: "I know of so many females who, the minute their boyfriend gives them a gun to hide, would yell 'Eek, get lost! But I've got to admit that when some wise guy first put a gun in my hand, it really turned me on!" "That's really sweet De" Sandra replied. "You know some females are just stupid bimbos, they try so hard to blend in, though when the chips are down they just stick out like a fuckin' sore thumb!"

Dahlia rebuked Sandra with one of her finest phoney

glares and pretentiously retorted: "You can go out and kill some goon but you do not swear in front of a female!" Simultaneously, just as though they had rehearsed the reply together many times, they chorused: "If a female swears, she is a *WHORE!*"

"*No! No! No!*" Sandra interspersed, "Say *putana*, it sounds less grungy than whore!"

Dahlia dipped her finger into the macaroni sauce cooking pot. "Speaking of whores" she rambled, "I once dated one of those younger guys from the Organisations Mid-West – you know the type, they open their mouths and money tumbles out. It's ironic how for the older guys their work is a way of life and yet for these younger guys it's exclusively a way to make money."

"One time he took me to the jewellery store. Just like we'd go in and buy yoghurt. He bought me a five thousand dollar ring. Pity his girlfriend back home, she should lay him more than once a week!"

PART 14

'Romanticheroic' (Part 1)

By mid-January 1971 Dahlia had just turned eighteen years of age and yet in less than three years she had experienced one scrunched up romance, two broken engagements and one shambolic marriage.

Altogether there had been too many precipitously painful adult experiences for a juvenile who was riddled with questions regarding her own sexuality, and in any event was far too young to know her own mind. However she always had been a canny person and by 1974 she was physically and emotionally someone to make people gasp. Everything changed and forever when the paparazzi got the big story about Dahlia they had been waiting for. It was perhaps the result of some trendy hokum whilst Dahlia was choreographing 'Shenandoah' on Broadway during 1975. There were several photographs (I hear) bandied around town with explicit indications of lesbianism, but it was the attempt and, in the fullness of time, the successful suicide of two cast members which finally fast-tracked Dahlia's career toward the bottom of the slope!

The NY Daily News reflected: "Miss Carriera's choreography is superb 'tis a pity about her strong line in reptilian charm." Whilst the NY Post was slightly more intense, if not somewhat brutally frank: "She may be in tip-top shape for some furtive female admirers, however, not nearly good enough for unalloyed adulation – but perhaps not bad enough for crucifixion, yet!"

*

It was late in the pm when Sandra and Dahlia took the night flight through from Miami to Toronto and 1976 had been an excellent year for them both.

Canada punches well above her weight piano-wise and Sandra was rated to be in a list of the 25 greatest Canadian classical pianists. In her somewhat short career Sandra had amassed a discography that's astonishing in both size and variety. Chopin, Debussy and back to Scarlatti and outwards to Busoni. Seeming there is nobody she hasn't played. "The Queen was home" as one reporter observed the next day.

In a way the scandal over Dahlia had now long diminished, but not the attention. Sandra felt a certain uncertainty (even guilty) over what she and Dahlia were doing. So much so her anxiety prompted her to casually dismiss *"We've been sleeping together for two years"* as they stood before a hastily corralled press. She continued, drying her eyes with a handkerchief. "Dahlia and I love each other and we want to get married as soon as possible." She was only telling the truth and the hysterical crowds at the Toronto airport had forever laid to rest any so-called legend about unflappable Canadians. Indeed the couple had to post round-the-clock bodyguards outside their three-room Royal Suite at the King Edward Hotel.

That evening they downed a pitcher of martinis. The Queen was indeed home and her public no longer needed to be reminded that Dahlia was indeed her 'consort'!

'Romanticheroic' (Part 2)

Once upon a time …

Two creative girls unexpectedly met and immediately fell in love. They became so devoted to one another it wasn't long before the Supreme Court, under duress, allowed them to marry.

They both still actively – and most purposefully – pursued their careers and enjoyed shopping, travelling and dancing together frequently. Along the way these two most extraordinarily versatile 'muscavados' uncompromisingly rubbed-out virtually any antagonist who, at the bidding of their family consigliere, it was deemed necessary to do so!

However, their homes were always kept exceptionally spotless, they hardly ever cooked (except for pleasure) and they both enjoyed Daiquiris and Margaritas at the end of a busy day at the office and never looked anything other than fabulous all of the time.

The end.

PART 15

Too Much Pontification!

HUMANKIND IS FUNDAMENTALLY a mystery and a lie. Reading between all of the untruthfulness, the white lies, the deceitful lies and the whole mendaciousness in general, perhaps we can obtain our only glimmer of truth in the relationship we find between the mysteries and not, as one would imagine, between the lies. For example, what of Chappaquiddick, mystery or lies? What of the First Lady of American ghosts, mystery or lies? Too late to ask Mary Jo or Norma Jean, yet not too late to realise that the very humanness of our species will be at stake unless we can throw away all of the absurd ideologies on which modern man has been crucified thus far.

Tall grasses, spiky thistles, briars were everywhere in the cemetery, crowding the crumbling rock of the headstones. It was a cold winter day in this neglected corner of nowhere yet Sandra and Dahlia utterly loved the divine wonderment of it all. "Gee it's old" Sandra yawned.

"Winter lies too long in these country towns, it just hangs on until it's shabby, old and sullen. Places like this bring out the spiritual feeling in you, don't you think?" asked Dahlia sort of cynically. "I am not against the killing of anything that lives, but I am committed to not bringing unwanted babies into the world. I have seen too many neglected, battered and mentally scarred kids. Unwanted children should not be conceived."

"So you are in favour of abortion?" Sandra enquired.

"Abortion would never be necessary if women stopped being so curious regarding some self proclaimed heart-throb – it's all down to being responsible, don't you think?" Dahlia replied.

Sandra dilly-dallied in her reply: "A person is killed in Hindustan – I feel the bullet. A child is crying in the street – its tears could be my own. A dead animal by the roadside – it stays with me for days, but if my zodiacs tell me I am only taking away the need of killing by killing someone who needs killing, that's all!"

Dahlia smiled lovingly at Sandra. "Let's get the lead out" she brashly sighed. Enough philosophising cowgirl, let's find Mom's casket and go home."

The girls and the day cared for Mom a lot, but she was dead and already her grave was beginning to be covered with ivy. The needy relatives, the negligent mooches, the ones who had missed the great opportunity to know her (instead of porch-sitting and missing the deadline) and all of the tiny blue forget-me-not notes – they had all been dispensed and dispersed. Sandra and Dahlia – they hadn't been here when she died – they were her steadfast lovers, yet they were the ones left behind and only here now out of out and out old-fashioned sentimentality. It was as though they were insulting her and that even in death Mom was expected to understand. How monstrous, how shocking, but Mom was never easily offended, at least not by 'her girls'. She was always quite cynical in any event and so the girls being here today (late though they may be) would have been really quite trivial to her!

PART 16

'Fellow Kooshdakhaa'

IT BECOMES OBVIOUS that you may like sharing your apartment with a ghost or two, when in this age of great communication satellites, fibre-optic data transmission, modems and so on, and so on, you very much prefer the connections that you have with your ghosts! There is no especial explanation for it except that perhaps the concept of having the so-called monopoly on such especial friends is a very precious privilege indeed for you. Any amalgam of fear that you may have from time to time is usually outweighed by your neediness to make acquaintance with folks on this level. It's not unlike preferring American cigarettes to British, they have a completely unique quality to them, or in preferring Coke to fruit juice for that matter.

There were many such phenomena in Sandra and Dahlia's brownstone tenement which they took no account of (Mom cautioned, "let the dead be dead"). However, of late things were beginning to come to a boil, but like a steam kettle which is whistling loudly they had chosen to ignore it.

It was mid-winter, just before Xmas, a strangely quiet looking day. Everything was so very normal on the surface – the children's melodic voices as they puttered to school, the tantalizing aroma of freshly baked bread from the bakers in the precinct, yet as they sat and drank their sweetened coffee together (a routine ritual) the peace and normative life seemed to have been, for the time being, temporarily sucked away from them by a whirlwind of total metaphysical proportion that had abnormally presented itself yesterday evening.

There are many pseudo-histories of the vampire-like chupacabra. As with Bigfoot, the Loch Ness monster and all the other beasts in urban legends, the tale of the chapacabra thrives upon the very active imagination of the public at large. It was the facts of this sagebrush subject that was occupying the copious chitchat as Sandra and Dahlia journeyed homewards after the sombre task of laying thoughts of Mom to rest. On these snow covered backroads it was never easy to make out the gulches on either side of the road – and Sandra didn't!

It seems to me that there are some pivotal points in a person's life when they fall down Alice's rabbit hole and find that afterwards everything has significantly changed. Right from the get-go of falling down that hole you become a different entity than you were before. With that concept in mind I would in all probability need a chapter to explain it, however, in brief here it is:

I guess they both figured that they'd stay topsy-turvy in their vehicle until perhaps a trucker came by in early morning. Keep the engine running, smoke their heads off and relax – that's a good idea!

When the north wind blows strong, the Iroquois say: *"The Bear is prowling the sky"*.

Now Sandra and Dahlia definitely lived on the border-land of death and spirits and so, entirely consistent with that observation, together with their character and their own philosophy of spiritual balance, it was for sure that someday 'change' would invariably catch them out! It's true, that in the loneliness of winter a person's imagination becomes reality in their mind! There comes a point when a mere blizzard can last more than a year, and when a person's mind is crowded even more by pack ice and simultaneously a bear shows up – shoot him or shoot yourself, it's all the same in any event!

However, this was not the situation, their needs meet which postponed or overcame death. Death only yielded symbolism of suffering and in the alchemy of the present the quest for life was greater than the circumstances. They had each other, and it was purely a matter of time before help arrived anyways.

Sandra cosied up closer to Dahlia. "Don't get weird on me Sandra" she wisecracked. "I am as unnerved as you!" Sandra steadily and intently looked at her. "Do you remember when on my birthday you crazily tap danced for me down 51st Street in Manhattan?" Dahlia half smiled. "I wouldn't have experienced that moment if Sandra my guardian angel hadn't shown up" she added. ""Didn't Clarence ever give you your wings for saving me that night Sandy?"

"Deliverance from that death, the death of the womb, is an entrance, a delivery over to another death"

John Donne, Death's Duel

Mom had her own favourable clarification to the normative and the nonsensical uncertainties of life:

"Pure and transparent like the clouds and the snow – no uniformity or shape are the Wendigo"

Some of Mom's accounts had a habit of conflicting with one another. In some stories they are cruel mischievous creatures who take delight in tricking poor travellers, in others they are friendly and helpful, frequently saving the lost and guileless from certain death and freezing. However, ultimately they always concealed their motive which was to transform their subject into a fellow Kooshdakhaa. A shape-shifting creature capable of assuming human form and so that incarnation of them would continue! Mom said that it was well known that many American Indians had occult powers and so it was fair to assume that these powers were passed on by the Kooshdakhaa.

Mom was unfailingly ever so careful regarding who she told, what she told and what she told to whom. In spite of that, the most important thing about her stories of inexhaustible inexactitude was all of the gaps and silences which momentarily were of crucial significance to outlast the night.

Death without doubt courts death. Dahlia and Sandra were especially daubed with its thick black substance. It was as though there were a metaphysical message being transmitted from them – a swirl of glints and angles, an aura that tumbles together and becomes tangled in the world of Genesis – a world balancing precariously on confusion, a world where distinct elements of shape and formity do not exist.

They watched the darkness in horror –

"Hello, hello, hello ... is there anybody out there ... out there ... out there?" Sandra's words seemed to take on a tormented echo. It was as though she neurotically felt the need to meet the perpetrator of their expendable lives – if that's what the overall purpose was. "Kill me, anything" she thought. It had always been one of Sandra's spaghetti ideals, either the quest for life or the immersion of death, to get into the spirit of things in other words!

As if by negotiation it finally showed itself, an indefinably impious plethora of frenzied iniquitousness and yet profoundly exotic with a raven black pelt covering its anarchic figure. It moved around and around and around their vehicle like a tempestuous cyclone, hesitating from time to time jabbing at the metal and glass as though teasing its protection.

It was one of those times when it gets so cold that even warm-blooded people can literally sparkle with icicles and when they do the demon can inflict additional chills in order to take full possession of that person's body. It is as though there becomes a natural spontaneous energy between you and it – a sort of merging with one another. An infuriating place in time, space, material, nature and many other limitative and irrational differentials, when as infinity dictates that you become inflicted to exhibit the same essential quality.

"In the bleak mid-winter, frosty winds made moan... Come to me in the silence of the night, in the speaking silence of a dream."

Christina Rossetti

From God the Creator at the top to so-called brute animals at the bottom, man's place is probably somewhere between the angels (immediately above) and the animals (immediately below). Since man was so-called 'created in the image of God, perhaps he has a kind and a rational mind, however, he is also subject to animalistic and irrational passions – so where did that come from? Whichever way you look at it, these are opposing forces and, depending upon whether his reason or passions get the upper hand, man will be either god like or bestial and women too for that matter! Never usually the hero, Dahlia always thought of Satan himself as a most interesting character. Inasmuch that he does have traces of self-assurance and panache about him!

For example:

His Satanic metamorphosis can adopt the form of a prowling wolf, a toad or serpent or indeed any animal whose sliminess and cunning can equal his own. Don't forget he even whispered his own 'Christian' virtues (and flattery) into Eve's ear!

Dahlia and Sandra were so fully aware that, unlike washing machines and automobiles, death cannot be superceded by a newer model. Unlike the quantitative sciences, there is no such thing as progress as far as death is concerned. It is not as we are taught, a theological or philosophical treatise which can be refuted if we so desire, it is final! Now, a critical reader must begin to understand the minds of Dahlia and Sandra (as well as their imagination) to accurately understand the conceptual framework of what they believe occurs after death.

Perhaps to understand the question we should know that the order and goodness of the world depends upon all creatures being in their proper places, which stretches to this creature being totally out of place! Then there was nothingness – it was gone. Dahlia opened her mouth to speak, then waited, hearing her own heart holding fast against the icy dark interior of the vehicle. She was struck by the darkness having such a direct correlation to the bitter sensation of cold and said so to Sandra as positively it did!

Looking out through the windscreen at the greenish-blue night Sandra uttered "It's gone, it's left us behind Dahlia – perhaps it's a token of its love for us after all?"

Dahlia's eyes brightened and she began to laugh – slightly a cackle because her throat had become dry, slightly a giggle because to her the whole thing had been such a 'fun run'. She stared at Sandra like she had had a recent revelation: "You look like Kim Novak in this light, with your hair all pulled back, perhaps we should dye it platinum, what do you think?"

Sandra remarked how the evening felt so Christmassy and began to sing:

"Deck the halls with boughs of holly
Fa-la-la-la-la-la-la-la-la
'Tis the season to be jolly
Fa-la-la-la-la-la-la-la-la
Don we now our…"

The sun was coming up over the horizon, looked like the day might turn warm – she just knew it would eventually!

PART 17

We Joined The Wild Birds In Their Crying And Carried On

YOU CAN LEARN so much, anything that you always wanted to learn, or so it seems when you are standing still on the ominous banks of the Kcnachdaw River. In winter the branches on the trees tremble with answers after dark. It's as though they wish to rid themselves of their secrets. If you hearken real attentively you will hear their personality crying out to you. We all grow small withered and somewhat circumspect on the extrinsically wily banks of the Kcnachdaw River in bleak winter on the far side of time.

Along the sidewalks of her imagination, where buffalo lay dying and the friendly dead are calling 'HELP!' and misspelled letters are coming back unopened, Sandra could see the storm was rising beneath her frowns and this was her opportune hour to fess-up, to reluctantly acknowledge and then to ever constantly 'move on' at a more beautiful pace.

Chowderheaded Fashionista

Dahlia joined the huddled masses boarding the bulging street car at Dundas & Vine. Sitting next to her was a middle aged, somewhat striking woman dressed with fur attire: coat, hat and dinky muffs. Dahlia leaned toward the woman and whispered almost lyrically in the woman's ear "thought I ought to let you know that your coat is still bleeding around the collar – there's a tiny red stream dripping over your leather boots – I think your hat may have haemorrhaged into your hair as well!"

Dahlia's tone contained a certain sureness in it; a kind of sureness that almost made you believe that what she was saying was factual. It was a necessary observation in any event and I guess that so were the 'daggers at dawn' scowl she got back. Dahlia illustrated the woman's 'look' to Sandra later that evening as "a plastic snow type of look – the kind of look that a Bible temptress might have given Solomon as she handed him some poison fruit."

"A switchback is such a lousy pretentious accessory to have to carry on a street car and they rust so rapidly without use" Dahlia concluded. "So on this occasion you slipped it back into your purse?" Sandra enquired curiously. "Yeah, I did" replied Dahlia "but only because that horrible woman reminded me of Minnie Pearl, and for that reason only."

"What about you Sandy?" Dahlia asked. "Did you find what you were searching out at Kcnachdaw River?" "Yes I did" Sandra beamed from ear to ear. "Loving you has made me not less optimistic, but far less systematic and I really like that new kind optimism."

"I only know how true it is; that love is a chain of love, as nature is a chain of life"

Truman Capote (The Grass Harp)

PART 18

Sexuality And The Killing Of Folk

As FAR AS Sandra and Dahlia were concerned, their puppet-play with such mundane and routine matters such as life and death was of little corrosive consequence. For them it was a source of freedom; not only from life's tediousness, but also as a means of escape from the tyranny that other folk tend to litter your life with.

With regard to their quiddity, they themselves were innate and somewhat intuitive puppet masters, and they themselves were able to exercise complete control over the whole performances. In terms of style, expression, spontaneity and vitality, now that was Dahlia's speciality (as I expected!), whilst Sandra's talent lay in the systematic way in which she could structure and co-ordinate the plan.

There was a remarkably bold simplicity that linked with what they did and why they loved it so much. Sure, at times things (situations) were to some extent illogical, nightmarish or even on occasion downright horrific. However, they both always had the ability to still give their 'subject matter' a certain style. Dahlia had always said that it was their 'arousing' style that indubitably singled them out from the notoriously narrow-minded monkey tricks of their competitors. Sandra told me that what makes them both so spectacularly successful is our unenlightened and sinfully unrealistic society. For example; (she drew this analogy for me) a young man and woman are expected to respond to each other's kisses. However, happy endings are for the birds, Sandra remarked with certainty. No one should expect that what promises to become love's happy ending is automatically just a matter of course. What makes us so spectacularly successful is that oftentimes love's happy ending is dramatically transformed into a spruced up nightmare!

For both Sandra and Dahlia the themes of love, frustration, life and death became the very embodiment of physical and mental desire during their infant years and on into their teenage years, particularly in their pubescent period – the years when the totally inexperienced suddenly discover the magic of love, yet in the process are also made aware of their inability to satisfy that love. The very experience of true passion thus has its own cruel powerlessness and frustration and inability. The heart-rending complexity of communication and effectively 'giving the game away' to the world around you. The so-called 'wrong' sexual tendencies, the tempestuous nature of isolation. The fostered sense of guilt – the aimless indiscriminate circle of trying to dissimulate every thought and every feeling.

One of the girls in Sandra's dorm had once confronted her directly with the question: "You're a bit of a queer aren't you?" Although Sandra hadn't had any type of relationship with anyone she was nevertheless disturbed and taken aback that her sexuality had become so obvious to a complete stranger. Dahlia too had experienced the self-same treatment and had accordingly stomped on the aspersionist's foot! – Dahlia could be a little too edgy at times!

In a kind of uncanny way, their friendship and eventual relationship just heightened the urgency of their tempestuous quest to bring about the end of the anguish of failure that this world dishearteningly distributes in such a casual manner.

These stealthy fireflies of feloniousness, whose exquisiteness will endure with the passage of time, these instruments of fate and death, of bitter social satire and of the muddy marks of the absurdity and futility of past worries.

Nowhere else in this novel is there such a combined projection of Sandra's and Dahlia's inner life and how it has manoeuvred and so the author has marked this decisive point as a kind of intermission in the evaluation of them both.

If indeed they have become so-called puppet masters, then it is indeed with some joy and charming innocence. In the puppet master's hands only the dead need to be friendly in any event!

PART 19

"Memory is a cemetery I've visited once or twice,
white ubiquitous and the set aside everywhere
under foot ..."

Charles Wright

DAHLIA HAD SPENT the last three and a half hours watching
Gone With The Wind – detached and unmet, as though it
had been especially written just for her. It always left her
glowing from the inside out as though there were no
more sensibilities left in the whole world.

"Do you suppose that's really a true account of how
things were back them?" she asked Sandra (as though
she needed some kind of substitute for reason). "I guess
it was the 'Old' South" Sandra replied – perched upon a
third pillow and wanting to sleep!

The station signed off – there was the waving of Stars
and Stripe and they cuddled down to sleep; a somewhat
strange parentheses framing the lives that they'll both
wake to, there huddled on the tiny island of bed and for
both 'quiet in the language of blood' for now.

The phrase 'an unfortunate incident' was a phrase that
Sandra used a lot. I remember once we were discussing
'The St Valentine's Day Massacre'; that was when I first
heard her use that phrase. I guess to most folk it was just
an indiscriminate slaughter, but Sandra always seemed
to have a knack of understatement where killing and
murder were concerned. On Sunday after Church we

visited a mulatto friend of the girls (she had a white Creole father). In this small Southern township words like 'peckerwood', 'nigger lover' and 'half breed' take shape on a daily basis. That evening we all sat huddled together in her tiny tinderbox of a house and discussed, among other things, the language of blood and blood-letting that came with and was caused by the muck of ancestry and such.

The oil lamps flickered around us. Our shadows became like dart glyphs on the walls of ashen recriminations. Dahlia pranced around the living room in her very own whirl of pulsating possibilities: she had always been the child with far too many questions – the endless *why?* and *why?* and *why?* … and *why not?*

The constellation of a million fireflies were flickering in her head that evening. Death was always a fair master to both her and Sandra and by morning when its flames had all dimmed it had made equals of us all.

"O magnet-South! O glistening perfumed South!
My South! O quick mettle, rich blood impulse and love! Good and evil!
O all dear to me!"

Walt Whitman

Some sympathetic Daughters of the Confederacy had approved the slaying due to the sexual molestation of a negro girl by an emigrant farm worker – "negro or other-wise, we look after our own" was their sure reply.

There are some fish darting among some bones in Turtle Creek and some tokens of history have been put to rest. When Nina Simone remarked "Everybody knows about Mississippi" perhaps in a way it wasn't purely a criticism but more of an appraisal?

There was often a wordless intercourse between the girls and me after a so-called contract was enforced. Sometimes it was obvious, like a raised thumb or two fingers held up (which once meant victory, then peace; in this instance either would be relevant!) I came to understand all of their strange gestures, however, their actual body language gave absolutely nothing away! I broached this subject with Dahlia once. She flung her head back and sort of randomly replied "Death stops all of the body language both in the recipient and the claimant. The soul is a journeyman for both parties and that cannot be seen at all!"

My childish vanity of thinking I knew the answer all along bugged me as I walked home. Dahlia had given me just an 'obvious' conclusion to my silly question …which resulted in a 'dead end' of my limited comprehension of such matters! It seems to me that Charles Wright wasn't far off the mark when he wrote "Memory is a cemetery […]". Truth be told I myself tend to use ink to keep a record of my life; in book form I can close it down any time I wish. Who would want the lure of memory in any event? It is too flawed and too changeful. I just long to be completely free from my remembrances ,not having a constant recollection is so much easier than to carry the great irony of past history with me.

I recall how Blondy Swanson and his long-standing compadre 'Uncle' Mike both laughed out loud when the Zapruda film was finally allowed to be seen by the public.

They knew it didn't matter one speck of an iota whether Alek J Hidell or Lee Oswald had supposedly purchased the Mannlicher-Carcano. What did matter is how history, just like that fake or fatal bullet, can intersect history both in its path and its final destination and we, are we not, the same in the hands of history's great master; destiny – perhaps I was beginning to understand Dahlia's logic after all?

PART 20

Dangerous Dan McGrew

(Alex Kramer/Robert Whitney – inspired by 'The Shooting of Dan McGrew' by Robert Service)
Kenny Gardner (with Guy Lombardo Orch)
(recorded 1949)

A bunch of the boys were whoopin' it up
At the Malamute Cafe
And the ragtime kid at the music box
Was a jazzin a tune that was gay
And back of the bar in a poker game
Sat a man that everyone knew
He was grim and cold, he was bad and bold
He was dangerous Dan McGrew

And while dangerous Dan was a-playin his hand
And keeping his eye on the game
You could see standing by with a gleam in her eye
And her hair just as red as a flame
A gal who was tall, with a face like a doll
And her fingernails painted blue
Oh, a gal who was tall, with a face like a doll
The Lady that's known as Lou

Then out of the night which was fifty below
And into the din and the glare
A man staggered in who was haggard and thin
And his face was filled with despair
Now he looked all around until he had found
The Lady that's known as Lou
And then the stranger turned
And his eyes they burned
On Dangerous Dan McGrew

Then suddenly wham! All the lights went out
And a voice cried "Die you must"
And the women screamed and a shot rang out
And somebody bit the dust
And then the lights flashed on
And the north-west mounted police
Came a-crashin' through
They drew their guns and they said
"Which one is dangerous Dan McGrew?"

And then somebody said "Well hi there!"
And skipped across the floor
A – one, two, skip,hand on hip
Right out through the open door
Now was it the stranger a-takin' his leave?
Or the lady that's known as Lou?
It was nobody else in this whole wide world
But dangerous Dan McGrew!

Could have been 'Jim Bluebell' Kenny Gardner was waxing lyrical about in the old days 'Why they'd called him by such an opulent name?' It was odds-on because of his purple face and the way in which his gut splayed-out and covered his belt. Jim had earned himself a reputation of being somewhat of a ghost, inasmuch to the attention he paid to disappearing after killing folk. However, due to his ill health of late, Jim was now only employed as a 'tidy up person'. Post-haste after a formulaic demise it was left to Jim to take care of the 'trail'. For example: if you've ever watched a western 'B' movie, it isn't long before you find the fugitive laying a false trail for the posse – in essence, that became Jim Bluebell's forte. It was quarrelled over whether or not he did such like during the uncertainty of events after the JFK assiduous execution – and they are still searching for the reasons today!

Of late, it seems that Jim had become somewhat too easy-going in his felonious profession and this lackadaisicalness had come to their notice and nettled his employers. And so recently, with that in mind, Jim received a subtle and precise advance caution ie a one dollar bill with George Washington's picture removed from it, denoting 'worthlessness'.

Jim had learned the alphabet, he knew the old language. It was time for him to go to bed early and bring a cup of milk in case the cat gets hungry in the night. A regiment of young fellas would be waiting out there and listening harder that he could hear. Jim Bluebell was over 70 years of age in any event and so quiet intact retirement was not such an insufferable option, was it?

PART 21

"Lyonnaise Potatoes And Some Pork Chops – That's The Way To Live!"

THEY NICKNAMED HIM 'Whispering Smith' after a real-life figure of legend back in the 1860s. The original 'Smith' was a railroad detective who earned the nickname 'Whispering' on account he was fast on the draw and always spoke in a low, hard voice. Our 20th century 'Smith' was neither hero nor heel, though certain of his envious contemporaries felt he was more the latter than the 'Smith' of legend. I guess the fact that he was a sort of ambiguous character was which most professionals were in any event.

The secret is that all of these professionals knew that the true mastery of power (and thereby success) is invisibility and that potentially visibility meant vulnerability. It was as though they were all endowed with some sort of God-given concealed compos mentis. I find their math most impressive. For example, they not only knew the whereabouts of each cadaver in Montreal and Toronto, but also they knew why they were hidden when they were hidden and which one of them had hidden them. This enforced shared data was the bosses canny assurance against any one of its operators 'ratting out' against the others!

Sandra, Dahlia, Mom Provenzano, Jim Bluebell, Uncle

Mike, Blondy Swanson, Whispering Smith and others – this is the way they enjoy life; their meticulous formula of how to deactivate death. Theirs was the savour of the appetizer rather than the meal proper. There isn't some sort of profound correlation or corrupt interrelationship between all of the aforementioned individuals. The only way I can describe it is they are all like passengers on an ongoing train, each in their own way waiting for the self same destination and hopefully a soft amen!

There are so many bewildering contradictions contained in the somewhat eccentric and innocuous character of these folk and so many anecdotal accounts of their transgressions that it becomes somewhat difficult to decipher which is fact and which is speculation. In some respects I try not to dig too deep (no pun intended!) Fundamentally it's less stressful for me and less chancy for them – and I am comfortable in knowing that I can continue to walk my dog through the woods! I consider myself as just a 'loss adjuster' of finalities and some actualities nothing more, even though some loquacious gossip may indicate otherwise!

This author's observation:

It seems to me that places do rarely change – Montreal and Toronto are no exception. However, the emotional changes can be significant and not always enjoyable. Most stunningly places will disperse to suit their populace. For example, a beautiful spring morning or a profound snow covered day will quickly be erased from conscious thought as though sensitivity is an inadequacy and may inhibit them in some unpractical way. However, it may be that in certain instances such 'changings' could actually enhance the person's psyche – depending upon which mind's-eye a person elects to use! – You choose!

PART 22

"Otto, Make That Riff Staccato"

WHEN I FIRST met Dahlia and Sandra one of the more immediate things that struck me about them was their poise and composure – they had a certain 'tranquility' that I didn't expect. I remember seeing Mount Shasta for the first time – the snow and everything was just as I expected it to be, whereas meeting Dahlia and Sandra for the first time was less about who they were and more about who they appeared to be; not at all as I had previously envisaged.

Their living room though radiated an intangible opulence of genuineness. A decoratively carved antique coffee table stood adjacent to a skilfully built Portland stone fireplace, overlooked by two large ebony bookcases which lined the length of two walls. A grand piano with hinged lid lifted stood attentively in the centre of the room as though it was eavesdropping on the whole vivacious scene; awaiting its command!

Sandra confessed that from time to time she enjoyed tinkling the ivories, however, this would only occur when Dahlia was totally in an appreciative frame of mind. I was soon to learn that these eye-opening dames had many ideas that were exceptions, not the rule. It is too much to ask that each man in his lifetime makes a single contribution that is both unique and useful and yet

Dahlia and Sandra, with their dark indifference, never fail to astound me.

Their dual identity sometimes teeters on a tightrope. Balancing always balancing, one foot before the other down the rails and roads, and yet always tied securely and only because their need for each other is far more than the need for themselves. Their methods are transference, gratifications, diversions and mid-week picnics! Avoiding (even in sleep!) tenuousness of conscience, despondency and so-called anguish.

What I find is complicatedly alien to me and I have no answer. It is the self-aggrandizement of their competence as they leisurely look through their binoculars and deem that their rifle is an insignificant point of reference!

PART 23

Nice Girls Don't Stay For Breakfast!

"A string untied
needs tying up
as every empty space
to merely prove
its own existence
needs walking through"
Rod McKuen (from 'Finding My Father')

THE PROBLEMS OF tomorrow and the history of the past, the fact that their job was dangerous had been something they had kept a closer watch on of late. Only when the telephone intervenes, when another nostalgic call of death comes, does any sign of a protesting tear disappear.

For Dahlia and Sandra they had discovered how to choose when everything they had chosen to choose was not enough. When they walked away from their showbiz lives the sheer voluptuousness of the post plausible absence of applause was immediately a huge hurdle.

I guess that show business for them was all about wanting to be loved, wanting to avoid rejection. 'Healthy' people rarely have such a need to be constantly reinforced with overt appreciation. 'Healthy' people can settle for more satisfactory, less stressful ways of expressing their contribution in life. 'Healthy' people don't need to find a substitute for that show business magic in order to be happy. Perhaps deep down they both had a symbiotic relationship with not only each other, but also with their demons of fear and death. Their creative minds now worked as a team to make their 'come lately' craft every bit as good as the stars they used to be – maybe more so.

Here they were, two women springing from completely different backgrounds, yet born into each others' lives and each sparring with the complexities of life and death and with the intricate impact they have on one another. They had one or two angry negatives from time to time, however, most were purged away by their daily workout – sometimes for up to three hours a day.

A little bit of pain was addictive to them. It was as though if by relinquishing that pain their 'performance' would somehow be impaired. Diet was as important as the correct exercise. At least eight glasses of water a day – their car rolled with plastic – Evian water bottles everywhere! And never eat dinner later than eight at night. Candy was a psychological reward, but not too much of it! It wasn't easy but it was perfect and the inexpressible feeling of gratitude for one another broke out of their souls and filled the room whenever you were in their company.

The wind rose out of nowhere that day, as the first crystals of snow arrived. Sandra was away for a couple of days visiting an old friend 'up state'. With Sandra 'elsewhere', Dahlia was beginning to feel so sexually unfrequented and somewhat bored. Cousin Tony had uncomfortably just walked down the aisle with Valeria whose belly protruded up and out, enough for everyone to recognise that another Guerriri was on its way! Perhaps it is a common affliction of so-called 'synergetic' persons of low intelligence yet here they were sat in Dahlia's living room two foot apart, like they weren't even players in the same symphony. Women in pastels and smelling of musk just elbowed Dahlia's sympathy for Valeria who was silent except for a few sniffles. Dahlia listened to them both jabbering on about their predicament. Like urine in the snow their love was sullied, blighted and not worthy of the tiny infant they had indiscriminately made. Dahlia's mind drifted – all she could think about was Sandra and their first Christmas together:

Women in love, walking home together from the dance. Both in ridiculous mini dresses. How perfect it was, the two of them trudging in the snow. Dahlia wanted to kiss her right there under the streetlight, but she was still hiding behind the farce of being afraid to show their love in public. They swayed down the street singing *Buffalo Gals* from the movie they both adored, their voices ringing like silvery bells in the frozen air of twilight. Clarence, their guardian angel, had undoubtedly shown up that night … and they promised him wings!

"In the people whom we love, there is, immanent,
a certain dream which we cannot always clearly
discern but which we pursue"

Marcel Proust

Dahlia took a deep breath and gazed at Cousin Tony and Valeria like they were just a natural disaster – like disease and war and more hypocrisy. "It's okay! It's going to be okay" she said. "Don't worry about it." She drummed her fingers on the counter impatiently, put on an Elvis Costello CD and made herself comfortable on her futon. Holding their hands tightly with her firm fingers clutching theirs, she hoped to feel excited, hopeful or even anxious by her decision, but she didn't and merely whispered, her doe-like hazel eyes glazed, "Sandra and I will have your baby and bring her up!"

PART 24

Aaron Slick From Punkin Crick!

"For that which befalleth the sons of men befalleth beasts; even one thing befalleth them: as the one dieth, so dieth the other; yea, they have all one breath; so that a man hath no pre-eminence above a beast: for all is vanity"

Ecclesiastes 3:19

FOR EVERY STAR that falls to earth a new one grows and for every dream that fades away a new one grows. Dahlia and Sandra were disturbed by such flapdoodle bunkum and could hardly imagine how such unreal sentiments existed. "It's a schmaltzy world – folks either take everything literally or spiritually, there is no in-between" was Sandra's estimation.

What was real was the red maples and blossoming orchards and the bright moon pasted in the sky – the feeling that 'uncertainty' was finally relaxing its hold and everything was falling wondrously into place. Women tend to play the villains in fairy tales, but not these two- either literally or spiritually! Yet, only a day and a telephone message away was a place where loneliness is unbearable. Where you are reminded to be a child again, a child who can't be left alone. If history is time travel, then this is a journey Dahlia and Sandra will never forget (let alone the smell!)

It took place in the wilderness, a place where wolves follow you home – a place that touches on what is unreal and yet by no means is untrue – a place that is forever unspooling itself in that fertile dreamlike expanse of the mind that lays mostly dormant between the uncanny and the absurd.

Groves of oak, mossy bogs and a tangle of streams; a chill of decay and death hung in the air that dark mid winter day.

Now Aaron lived in the most malignant squalor imaginable, not as a result of his poverty, purely as a result of his own neglect. His home had passed the stages of easily understood muckiness, though perhaps his slovenliness indeed had even passed the stages of disgusting. When a person lives in conditions this bad it can only be described as 'demonic' – indeed poor Aaron was somewhat half human and half demon; a kind of 'necromancer' raised from the dead. You might say a certain kind of horrible entity who could afflict mankind with plague and pestilence just by them entering his home … and yet he was a lovely fellow if you were able to ignore (and step over) the poo-turds on the carpet and the environmentally unfriendly viridescent and airless dwelling he lived in. He perpetually walked up and down as though he was unable to rest until the mountain of recriminations he had imposed upon himself were told. After telling the girls his story his relief was all too apparent. His eyes held their gaze, there were no gestures of anxiety from him any longer – he knew that everything else would follow the normal course of events – it was just another surgical operation!

Aaron's tale as told to Dahlia and Sandra:

Nearly three years had passed since my wife's death and yet, as I was passing through a somewhat second-rate area of Toronto, I came face to face with a lady in whom I recognised as none other than the wife whose death I had mourned for so long. As I attempted to speak she averted her looks and swept past swiftly and was driven quickly away by a cab before I could reach her. It was a difficult task to obtain an order for the grave of my wife to be exhumed and to be examined – nevertheless I did obtain an order and the empty coffin turned suspicion into certainty. For whatever reasons I had been suckered, wandering through a nightmare of her assumed death for years and now I wish to buy for her a 'true' death, too beautiful to describe – the necessities of her life finally perceived by real live worms!

On their long journey home Sandra subtly contemplated: "I guess his wife gave him a lesson in rejection." Dahlia emphasized a sniff and replied: "Yeah, but she didn't figure on that second-rate area of Toronto as being the 'whole' world!

PART 25

Double Entendre (Entarndra)

"I carry your books – I give you looks that say 'I
love you'
I send you flowers – spend my hours just thinking
of you
But I saw you late last night
You were holding another boy tight
Go ahead explain, but remember if you lie
The Bogeyman will get you and your nose is
gonna grow
So remember if you lie
Everyone will know.
You're holding my hand making plans to stay
together
Promising me that our love will be forever
If everything you say is true who's the boy I saw
with you?
Go ahead explain, but remember if you lie
The Bogeyman will get you and your nose is
gonna grow"

Johnny Crawford

THE WORD 'INGENUE' doesn't exist in the English language
for a male counterpart to the female usage of 'ingenue' –
although it should. Nonetheless the word 'greenhorn' is
a somewhat gender neutrality aphorism and that was in

essence what I was. 'Wrenchingly' optimistic also springs to mind! However, there comes a time when the heart's beat has had enough of pseudo romantic love affairs. The involvement as such is too full of bruises and lies and absolutely nothing else.

A bizarre thing happens when it's twenty below zero outside and you are relaxing warm and cosy with friends talking about destiny and all sorts of other philosophical stuff. Sometimes things just appear out of the woodwork that you truly never expected. I guess that is one of the unique weaknesses of being with friends you can really trust. I had nicknamed their home 'the house of death'. Neither of the girls objected, in fact Dahlia had remarked that it was a "charmingly British colloquialism – kind of cute and endearing".

I loved these girls and they loved each other and me. I loved these especial evenings, not because we rarely spent them together, but because we all shared the same fear, the same cruelty, the same future, the same ashes and dust, ashes ...

About the time that you find love, about the time that you pay some mind to it at all, the summer may be gone and you may go home alone. About the time that you find yourself wondering what all the shouting's been about, you may find it's about time, about the time after all. When finally love shows its other side as it has a tendency to do, be careful not to title it 'hate'.

A bizarre thing happens when it's twenty below zero outside and you are relaxing warm and cosy with friends. You tend to get a different perspective on life's biography, especially regarding being cheated on or being given the big E! My inner self was asking me, Ricky, why did you do it? Without a good reason you risked being tried for murder in the first degree. You know what the penalty is for that in this state? Hanging! Now just smarten up and convince me why it was necessary, if indeed it was!

A concealed voice replied "I killed her and that's the end of it. In any event why *not*?"

In actuality 30,000 dollars was the amount agreed upon. Truth be told that is not a great wad for two connoisseur practitioners who were not soggy sentimentalists at heart as I am. Although the thought of it gives me a nice troublesome ulcer from time to time. However, heart attacks are so commonplace, don't you think?

PART 26

'Shanghai Lil'

THE COST OF one warm moment is considerable and whatever small kindness or of light it brings it may unwittingly demand an unknown spirituality in you that you never knew you possessed.

No matter how, by fair means or foul, a little lost bird may arrive one day on your doorstep of lifetime experiences. So ashamedly alone, so rancorously forgotten and so absolutely unwanted. Knocked down by the wind, scathed by the mizzle of blood stock, its destiny will be yours. Should you choose to turn and walk away, or should you take its tiny life in your cupped hands and bid it to stay until it grows wise and mature? The verdict is yours, and you cannot ever go back. You reach out; for what is life without a little bird song?

Well, it's never warm enough, it's never cold enough: if you wake her to feed her she cries, if you don't wake her she cries anyway! Her brain is still an embryo and your brain is fast becoming one. She can't form sentences yet and you can't even form words. She can't even make a fist and for that matter neither can you, yet she is quite big enough to always be getting in the way and you ... you have become irrelevantly peripheral! On a two to one basis that's what Dahlia and Sandra especially enjoyed about being parents to baby Guerriri.

Cousin Tony and wife Valeria had quickly and efficiently done the handover to Dahlia and Sandra and scarpered with the incredulity of a monkey with a hard-on. It wasn't that they were upset or even slightly distressed at either the thought, the practicality or the final implementation of baby Guerriri's giveaway, or indeed anything at all of an emotional nature. If anything, they seemed somewhat relieved. For that matter Dahlia and Sandra also felt a certain 'mental' repose now that the deed was done – so to speak. However, in spite of all the anxious comings and goings both girls realistically agreed that they felt unable to summon up or to suggest that they felt any sort of maternal awareness regarding baby Guerriri's nurturing, although they both promptly agreed regarding the intangibly uncanny excitement that this new responsibility had afforded them with.

There was no matter of fact explanation relating to the child's untypical Eurasian likeness though, inasmuch that its natural parents originated from southern Italy. However, regardless of the 'replicant' and wherever the ethnic thing had evolved, all that was decisive was the cutting of the child's umbilical link to the Guerriri's once and for all.

They watched her sleep, her tangled black baby hair soft on a white pillow.

"We will charter new and beautiful worlds for you baby ours," Sandra murmured softly.

Dahlia responded, her low voice filled with certainty. She added "… for you to confidently walk and love in".

*

I'd hoped that by now I might have learned the rationale behind their choosing a name for the little mite. However, I haven't yet. Decidedly they named her 'Shanghai Lillian' – that indeed was love's name! Some oxymoron eh?

PART 27

It's A Rainy Night (In Georgia)

Instructions 1 of 6

THERE TENDS TO be a sacrilegious v Oltenian nimbleness with regarding delivering the fatal hit and getting the fuck out! Losing all trace of yourself must fly with the speed of light from 'hit' toward the absolute 'O' swiftly and proficiently; the remainder is restful silence. There is never a reason or explanation for that restful silence – you care zilch for its syllables, you only care for the silence itself.

The hush hush secret is to compress the 'targets' world to the size of a bumble bee, which you, the thrush swallow (the bird of death!) and sever their umbilical link to this world forever. No one sees the unseen hand of death when it comes calling and you can bet your Bible on that! Dahlia and Sandra were mightily effective 'jobbers' who always achieved what they wanted. However, what in doing so they risked losing what they had. A somewhat dippy dilemma and for the first time in their accomplished profession they were struggling for a solution!

People grow old and people grow tired and somewhat absent-minded, particularly when it suits their own agenda. It is as though they choose to almost forcibly become forgetful, or do they feel that 'others' may forcibly improve their forgetfulness to endure?

Take for instance what the Persico family did to murder and tyrannize their way to the top of the Organisation and create a billion dollar empire for themselves. Take for instance how Bernadette Provenzano had remained dumb and blindfolded whilst her sister Griselda Persico had assembled a private army who would execute all competitors along the way. However the 'inexplicable' disappearance of Griselda after facing twelve charges including drug trafficking, obstruction of justice, money laundering and murder was a significant message that Bernadette was not about to die of natural causes. It was all about enforcing family discipline and Bernadette was a kind of unintentional loose cannon in the most dysfunctional family in the United States. There had been some forty-year delay, but now the piper would unavoidably have to be paid, or so it would seem!

I cannot remember Dahlia and Sandra as having that many special female friends. Strongly prodigious friends were, needless to say, Mom and Kim. Consequently, on the presupposition that Bernadette Provenzano appears to be a second cousin to Mom and Kim, that makes her into a special friend also. Be all that as it may, the overriding factor in this instance is the cablegram that came banging on Dahlia and Sandra's door. Its message was clear, comprehensible and toxic – "Bernadette Provenzano must not set eyes upon another whole winter." Their 'chief executive' had little bond with common speech, although he was not really a complicated man, Latin or Sanskrit the translation was never sympathetic in nature!

Forethought 2 of 6

Late autumn, October was flowing out onto the street. The sky violet, writing withering rays of sun upon the edifices of stone and latticed park benches. Hands caringly grasped together, yet not clouding their ability to think clearly regarding the matter in hand.

They weaved briefly away from the park path through an empire of rich golden and amber leaves, crunching and kicking them into the air like they were corn flakes. They adored these autumn rambles, jackets hanging loose, blowing gently, catching the slight chill of the watery twilight and just being so in love.

Faced with such a perspective of today's events, today they were like soldiers on their autumn manoeuvres. Loitering yes, but also thinking, assessing and considering. Their activities v regular folk – the oddness, the wrongness, the difficultness; nothing, absolutely nothing was easy and normal!

Special Delivery to Bernadette Provenzano:

Dear Butterfly

Forgive us, but we had to write to you – you are really on our shoulders every single moment lately. First and foremost we need to speak to you about an annoying family matter very soon, in fact sooner rather than later is recommended. Now that Griselda is off missing, we need to think about **your** safety and comfort. The final choice will be yours of course, but we implore you to CHOOSE WISELY!

Second, it's freezing here in NY – so we're heading South to see you (warmer climes) in Georgia within the next few days which will allow us a much deserved vacation as well!

With a wink and a whistle:

Dahlia and Sandra.

Her lip trembled involuntarily – Bernadette gazed teary-eyed at the letter. Was darkness covering the truth, how ambiguously was it written? Her eyes moved away and she lifted her head to gaze intently at the night sky and tried despairingly to locate her usual lone star that she had always relied upon. It seemed that her world was balancing so precariously upon whether or not to accept or believe that things are what they appear to be. She had heard various whispers regarding Dahlia and Sandra's clandestine operations and prayed that there was going to be more behind that letter than their Polish Italian intermingle of words or indeed the dineros!

The Meeting 4 of 6

It was showery and damp by the time they began entering the Atlanta area which was unusual weather for that time of year. I guess it was only momentarily because in the twinkling of an eye, by the time they neared Marietta, the sun was beaming away like nothing wet had happened.

Sandra loved mid-week picnics and pulled over to pick up some watermelons and tangerines from one of the many vendors at the roadside – offered by the sack not by the pound!

Eventually they took the last turn off past Chattahoochee Creek and drove some twenty bone-shaking miles down a back country track to Bernadette's farm and the middle of nowhere!

Bernadette skipped off the front porch joyously to greet them. She looked pretty much older than they both remembered, although ten years had passed since they had last visited her, but she was one of those ladies that no matter how old they became they would still look as prepossessing as a bouquet of posies in any event.

A neighbour passed by in his truck and gave us a perky wave. Southern hospitality and dust from his truck tyres knows no bounds in Georgia!

Bernadette had this captivating yet so offbeat way of drawling Dahlia and Sandra's first names into two syllables, it was almost as though she had momentarily forgotten to remember the second part!

The joie de vivre in the South gives rise to the slow melodious talk, the languid afternoon naps and perhaps the controversial confederate flag also takes a flutter! In any event this has got to be some idyll, just being idle.

Makes you feel as though you never want to go home to the North again where you have to be altogether too civilized to be civilized at all!

So they rested, listening to that old familiar Georgia rain again. Dahlia with one fractious cat (she liked cats), Sandra with Maria the duck (Maria liked Sandra) and Bernadette with her introspection!

The freckled day was moving into evening now and Bernadette had assembled a nutritious fricassee complete with grits! They were all chortling about nothing in particular. Perhaps it was just the joy of being in that moment, or perhaps it was the precipice that they were all conscientiously falling and hitting from one side to the other again and again and 'gittin' nowhere. The truth is that 'precipice' didn't stop the frogs or crickets, it didn't stop the barking dog in the distance and it didn't even stop the leisurely climbed back country singer on the radio. It most importantly didn't stop the never-ending offering of manly toasts to one another and all and sundry for that matter. The South Australian wine which Bernadette had acquired from the food market in Marietta was a great supplementary to the evening's superficial merriment that was for sure.

Ultimately, in the fullness of time, it was actually Bernadette who found the pluck to broach the unpleasant issue. "I die daily" she plunged right in; "wondering if tonight will be the night which the crickets will stop their adding and counting – and we can both sleep at last." She addressed the girls in a kind of 'happy go lucky' manner. "Neckties and petticoats, pistols and tennis and tea, I admire your grit – no room for faint-heartedness eh?"

She gazed at them fortuitously. "Do what pleases you, but be honest with me, is another day making ready to arrive or is there (for me) only night to follow?"

Suddenly they came to a gulf across the road. This one was so broad and deep that they knew at once they could not leap across it so they sat down to consider what they should do and after serious thought they concluded:

"Here is a great tree, standing close to the ditch. If we can chop it down so that it will fall to the other side, we can all walk across it easily."

"That is a first-rate idea said the lion. One would almost suspect you had brains in your head instead of straw!"

Adaptation from L Frank Baum's The Wizard of Oz
(first published in the 1900s)

Mom and her extended family always had a way of maintaining balance, even though they were constantly getting knocked about. Puts me in mind of the red-n-white striped buoys in the Niagara River which stand up so resiliently under the constant flow of water coming from the great waterfalls upstream. Now Dahlia, Sandra and Bernadette were amongst them; often fearful that they may sink under the pressure, but never allowing their smiles, winks and love to ever lack its lustre.

It seemed to me that both Dahlia and Sandra had collectively fallen head over heels in love with Bernadette – I would no double stifle that observation if asked point blank, however in reality there is no other way to interpret all of their frivolity of late.

I'd often take time out to watch their skylarking when-ever I had a few minutes to spare in the early morning before I'd leave for work: bouncing baby Lillian, laughing, joking and sharing oodles of French toast and the late City Final of the New York Post!

Oftentimes they'd spend an entire afternoon sat amidst the rose trees in Central Park just watching some kids play volleyball or such. On the face of it we were once and for all a beautifully joyful family. What was very unnerving was the desire that this happiness would go on forever ... could it!?

Home was indeed a fabulous place to be. The aroma of stewing tomatoes, fresh basil and oregano, the fragments of pine-scented furniture spray and a smile with an apron about her when I finally returned home in the evening – even the diapers drying on the overhang in the bathroom had a kind of simplistic nicety about them.

I did have some unspoken qualms at first regarding the domiciliary of certain indubitables, namely 'Maria and Fractious'. However, to tell you the truth they kind of grew on you and undoubtedly added a homespun rustic quality to city life!

All in all I would guess that it's a good sign of airiness when you begin taking the stairs from the lobby two at a time, no matter how ill-conceived that airiness is! In the summertime of days we are as we must be and can ask for nothing more besides.

Frank McErlane in 1931 shot his common-law wife and her two dogs and was never prosecuted, although The Outfit retired him on a small pension!

Bugsy Siegel once remarked inaccurately that "We only kill each other" – as though that makes it ok!

Colombian drug Lord Pablo Escobar once described himself as "a decent man who for the most part exports flowers!"

Illumination and imagination, death and rebirth, take their words if you will and fill in the blanks – however, on the seventh day of some seventh month the truth will out but until then my lips are for good and always sealed frozen!

The Associated Press report:

MORE THAN 50 FIRE FIGHTERS BATTLED A BLAZE AT AN ISOLATED FARMHOUSE IN NORTH FULTON COUNTY YESTERDAY. IT IS FEARED THAT THE OCCUPIER MISS BERNADETTE PROVENZANO PERISHED IN THE FIRE. HER TWO COMPANION ANIMALS SEEM TO HAVE ALSO LOST THEIR LIVES. FIRE CHIEF RAFFAELE SALERNO SAID IT WAS A MYSTERY HOW THE FIRE STARTED.

Once upon a time in a very different world, somewhat remote from smoke ashes and uncertainty, two plus one people were doing all they could to ensure the permanency of these very ephemeral moments. For example 'Bernadette Provenzano' was almost as thick and prevalent a name as a first Montana snowfall! In addition 'Bernadette Provenzano' was the moniker of a supposedly dead person and definitely dead in the event that the truth about her was ever discovered. With all those inescapable facts in mind, a brain-storming session decided to 'bury' Bernadette Provenzano and exhume 'Penny Penniman'.

Footnote:

It was Bernadette who suggested the parodic name as an acknowledgement to her idol Little Richard – birthname Richard Wayne Penniman, "born and raised in Georgia" she proudly added!

PART 28

What Is A Totemic Occurrence?

"Girls often have to be brave, resourceful and bold, indeed the private lives of girls are often colourful and surprising"

Louisa May Alcott

I GUESS THAT for Ivana Zelničková Winklmayr her 'totemic' moment came at the Montreal Olympic Games in 1976. Raised in Czechoslovakia under communist rule who could have ever predicted that sort of happenstance?

As for me, my 'totemic' experience was a much more profound event. A 'Damascene' moment of unrivalled revelation and downright independence is really the only way in which I dare describe it.

Without warning I became kind of 'metamorphosed' after a chance run-in with Dahlia and Sandra. Following through, here is the (almost) unelaborated testimony of that unusual encounter and our subsequent unique connection:

It was a pretty handscrabble life after the war, but our mother was an enduring woman and we got by. Our Ukranian father was about as abusive and Dickensian as they come and when he was home from the sea we learnt to avoid him. Our 'home' was a bug infested tenement flat in a block which stood alone surrounded by bombed and devastated buildings which Hitler hadn't missed.

My brother Mike and I nicknamed it 'Termite Terrace'. After my mother's death, my father vanished somewhere up north. Far as Mike and I were concerned it was a relief being rid of him. We grew up kind of half hitched, but happy in our raggedy and moderately bibulous way.

Mike was a wayward boy and as he was my younger sibling I was for evermore stepping in to help him if some geezer got out of line, but eventually Mike grew up and went on to marry a beautiful Sicilian girl called Angelica Vizzini. Mike sorts out problems or difficulties for the 'Family' now – he's known affectionately as Uncle Mike, the harbinger of every trouble, that's Mike!

Call out to a passing stranger, say hello, bonsoir. The no-more stranger in return will give a like greeting to another who will keep it going until the circle comes full circle again. That's pretty much how the run-in with Dahlia and Sandra came about for me. Fundamentally, Mike made 'me' known at an ad hoc gathering for his godchild (said I was a writer, etc) and I just simply 'circumambulated!'

I could never have imagined in my wildest dreams that I could live so well as I have with Sandra and Dahlia. I would have thought that their unusual entrepreneurism would stand us apart, however I have become part of them. There is no single day or time within the new life I have chosen that I'd have changed or altered. Possibly there are some days I could have missed and never missed, but I suspect that I could not have come down to this special place where I am in a different way. Truth is, as yet I don't know exactly where I am, but I am enjoying it immensely.

Even more incredible is how the 'Family' have accepted me, or so it seems. However, that still remains a little unclear and slightly ambiguous to answer. You see, within the Family there is an obligation to tell the truth, but there is also great reserve and this reserve, the things that are not said, rule like an irrevocable curse over the whole family. It makes all relationships profoundly false, perhaps even absurd. For example, if family member 'A' tells family member 'B' that he has assassinated or has terminated politician 'X' what he says is probably true. If it is not, then it is a tactical lie that, in its own way, is every bit as significant as the truth! The Family have many layers and each layer has its own important and relevant consequences, that's how I see it anyways.

One of the many enchanting qualities with regard to Dahlia and Sandra's total professionalism is their ability to put themselves in your shoes, to be in tune with your feelings. So when I had decided upon a suitable demise for my father, the only thing I had to take care of was the funeral itself. They say that a person's physiognomy is seen as an indication of their character and I know that to be true because he was and is a SOB. Like the day he presided over a sweepstake among his junior colleagues regarding the size of his own private parts – I do wonder if Pastor Parcelle would have enthused about that in his eulogy?

There were no shouting of hallelujahs to an unseen choir or demon-bashing oratories of long buried secrets to make his life seem more 'saintly' than it was. At best there was Pastor Parcelle's own generic choosing of Kipling's ditty *"If you can keep your head [...]"* speedily followed by the casket being lowered downward into the flames. Mike smiled smugly and wisecracked "told you he'd go down and not up".

Kim who'd overheard Mike's quip instantly cracked-up and was obliged to quieten her amusement by bunging her hand over her mouth.

Pastor Parcelle had effectively assumed that Kim was shedding tears of grief and so the whole shebang ended fairly well indeed!

For my part it was as though a new kind of freedom had arrived and found its roots in me and as for my father, well he had had a lot of everything in his wretched life. A lot of everything that's not worth reflecting upon let alone commemorating.

He invariably was a sardonic bastard and therefore the pure poetic justice of him choking on foie gras which resulted in a heart attack was an ending as ironic as sardonic can get!

PART 29

Funny How Blood Stains Clothes But Washes Off Hands

In 1920, 'Big Jim' Colosimo was ready to settle down. After years of running brothels and dope he had fallen in love with a beautiful brunette opera singer called Dale Winter. Their subsequent marriage lasted less than a month and ended with Colosimo's murder on May 11th 1920.

To this day it has never been officially established who actually fingered Big Jim, but in many respects marrying singer Dale Winter had led indirectly to Big Jim's demise. It seems he was becoming respectable. The association with Dale had even led to him hiring a tutor to teach him to speak correctly but, whilst cultivating the friendship of 'society', he was neglecting his 'business' companions! Al Brown was a brothel pimp who Big Jim had upgraded to make him a minor bodyguard to him. Al Brown was one of the aliases used by Alphonse Capone and, with that in mind, I wonder if Capone may have been instrumental in the big fellow's murder? In any event he lost no time in stepping into his shoes!

Tall grasses, spiky thistles, briars were everywhere in the overgrown and overcrowded cemetery. It was a bitter February for sure, so cold that even the evergreen ivy on Mom's headstone just crumpled like crazy when

I yanked at it. I'd brought a tiny nail brush with me to clean off the stone a bit, so as least Mom's name and other inscriptions were discernibly conspicuous. The lettering was inexpressive and simplistic, it read:

Dale Colosimo (Mom) 1901-1989
'WHEN IT COMES TO DYING, MOM KNOWS BEST'

I have clear deep images in my mind of the last time I saw Mom. She was a short genial looking lady who just resembled a quintessential elderly aunty. Not at all austere in either appearance or manner, yet she was still head of the Organisation from Toronto Heights and all points to the west. She greeted me with an explosive string of staccato Italian and shook my hand profusely. We participated in a bottle of her home-made liquor (which felt as though it could blow your head off). She was lovely. Her grammatical English was perfect, just marked by a heavy accent, that's all. She told me that her story came under the classification of 'old business' ventures and I guess it just did!

PART 30

Send In The Fools – 'Clowns'

(A retrospective look at Dahlia and Sandra's beginnings – embracing Sondheim's poetry)

Isn't it rich?
Aren't we a pair?
Me here at last on the ground
You in mid-air
Send in the clowns.
Isn't it bliss?
Don't you approve?
One who keeps tearing around
One who can't move
Where are the clowns?
Send in the clowns.
Just when I stopped openin' doors
Finally knowin' the one that I really wanted was yours
Making my entrance again with my usual flair
Sure of my lines, no one is there.
Don't you love farce? My fault I fear
I thought that you'd want what I want
Sorry my dear
But where are the clowns?
There ought to be clowns
Don't bother they're here.

Isn't it rich, isn't it queer?
Losing our timing this late in our career...

Footnote:

She's singing to the love of her life who isn't wanting to take them seriously. In the past she has always been the aloof one, but now he's the one floating around.

She finally sees that all she ever wanted was him, but he doesn't get it. She knows she's a fool, but cannot bring herself to move on.

She has always been aloof and noncommittal, she always knew what to say, but now she finally wants him, but it's too late, he's moved on and has someone else and she is left alone with memories of them and regret for not seeing it in time.

Although it's her fault, he's as much a fool as she. Now clowns needed since they're clowns too.

Love makes us all fools in the end, our maturity does not save us from heartbreak.

...love can make all of us fools and in the end even our maturity or past experience cannot save our souls from heartbreak. Here they were, Sandra and Dahlia, an anomaly of antithetical opposites – both with their own glaucous tomorrows, either left or owed, either borrowed and as yet unbought. Both transcending toward the heavens, or at least above the earth somewhere. Both unmindful of their suppressed mindfulness for a proper stranger's arms, each unpleasantly hovering somewhere between the popcorn and the flame. Each not wanting to take the other seriously, both aloof and preferring instead to secretly protect themselves in a safe place called 'non-committal'.

Dahlia, who has found the limit to how many changes a person can go through between her first love and the one who may burst her heart – and with those changes a kaleidoscope of differing views, sober and drunk. Sandra, who had metamorphosed in as a bitch goddess, since a bit of teenage rough and a one-night stand were the first and final grope that excommunicated her completely. Time and timing's everything and what they both have in common is an inexpressible sense of time. Alas a single minute lost is never made up and yet they fear that perhaps the kindness they've discerned as love is limited. A pity since even as they float around aimlessly the end is approaching fast and perhaps it's time to tear away the final cover.

I guess to be guilty only of some dark suspicions is not necessarily uncomfortable or wrong, on the under-standing that those dark suspicions pertain to yourself and provided that you recognise them for what they are (suspicions) and in the long-time perhaps they can be proved wrong. Withal 'suspicions' are only made up of memories and regret and for not seeing things clear at that time.

It really stings of dubiety to divvy up who is to blame – a fool is a fool is a fool. Love is a fool and makes us all fools in the end. Once I thought that they were exception, not the rule, but that is not so. The only regret is not seeing it in time and moving on, but in the wrong direction.

Touches not tradition are the only way forward for those willing to volunteer everything. Not necessarily in a literal sense. We don't have to touch to be touching nor walk together and be knowing that walking back will make the distance even better. The first night in, the first night out, of finding peacefulness mixed together with euphoria and giving over to your reborn beloved that one important facet of yourself that had been held back and afraid to give in the past. Doppelgangers who had been searching for their stopping place, a place removed from real time, a place where a tingle doesn't sting any longer.

'Concertedness'... mid-week picnics in Central Park, restraining from cussing in traffic congestion, cleaning out their closets together and squeaky clean washing each other's backs. They had listened to every stop-start motion of each other's lived-in lives and now whatever time it takes for them to muddle out and liven up, they had that time. Taking time out to be smitten with one another, to get off on it, not in an obsessive manner, more like intense enthusiasm!

Caring and being devoted enough not to hold on too tightly yet always making certain not to run too loose.

They both revealed that optimism kind of frightens them of late yet the necessity of being faithful without the complication of optimism is more realistically like telling it like it is.

It seems to me that it's all like a 'coming of age' for Dahlia and Sandra; there are some sentences that as yet they are unable to form. Taking time out to love is what they are really all about and the watching world should note that even the truest lovers need time to say love's name, wouldn't you agree?

PART 31

Contagion

MOM HAD TOLD them that she believed the cure for thinking too deeply about yourself and your own contractual obligations was to help someone who was far worse off than yourself. It ought to be added that that sort of cheesy sentimentality was faring less than well half a century later. It seems to me that those old patriarchs have long since turned to stone and their exemplar values along with them. Perhaps there was an air of sanctimoniousness in those moth-eaten ideals in any event, who knows? Adapt, amend or merely to remain indifferent, it is doubtful it really matters which way you interpret it. A means to an end is its all-important essence and perhaps a tinge of honour? Mom often referred to the right of a person to deal with their own problems without the help of anyone else and in particular a law-body; she called it the 'Omerta'. I did some research which lay bare the background or ancestry of the 'Omerta' per se. In a century of change it too is becoming a relic from a bygone age. Honour is unfortunately being silenced. It is impracticable and unreal. Money however talks prolifically!

I remember Mom making her voice kind of casual as she asked "If you are going to kill someone, first think about killing yourself. How would you do it?" She pressed on "I'd probably blow my brains out with a gun because

I wouldn't have a single clue as to which part of me to shoot at otherwise." Straight from the shoulder Mom continued "You oftentimes read in the tabloids about people who'd tried to shoot themselves, only they end up shooting an all important nerve and getting paralysed, or blasting their darn face off, but being saved by surgeons and it being proclaimed as some sort of miracle." She added "Just be certain that the poor mennonite gets an accommodating valediction, that's all!"

Rikers Island Prison was a little community and like most others it was run on its own rules and understandings. There was every sort of prisoner there, from simple robbers to terrorists and most of them abided by a rigid code of conduct. Grasses and informers were not tolerated and they usually finished up on Rule 43, which means they were constantly under the protection of the prison officers. However, an officer could often be bribed to be 'distracted' for the thirty seconds or so it took to punish a con who needed correction. Such was the son of Salvatore 'Toto' Riina Antonino. A ruthless assassin who was mirroring his late father, or at least trying to.

Dahlia was chock-full of sass. "How d'yer get into that prison?" she quizzed the guard. "You get a pass" he smilingly replied. "No!" she continued "how do you get *locked in*?" "Oh!" the guard laughed "you steal a car, you rob a store." "You got any murderers in there?" Now Dahlia was in full flight! "No, murderers go to a big place up state." Dahlia just kept askin! "Who else you keep in there?" "Well, during the winter we get these old bums, they heave a brick through a glass window just to get picked up and spend a few months out of the cold – you know, TV and plenty to eat." "That's sweet" she replied smiling. "Nice if you can get it" said the guard drolly.

She eventually bid him goodbye and moved off at a lively step toward town to meet with Sandra over a liquid lunch at the Royal Oak Lounge. She glanced back over her shoulder only once. The guard was stood in the doorway of his observation booth with a kind of speculative look on his face and as she turned he lifted his arm in a humorous salute to her.

"I'm going to masquerade as a psychiatrist" Sandra spoke with her usual breathy enthusiasm over such matters. Sandra and Dahlia were enjoying pear cider in the Royal Oak Lounge – they were very fond of pear cider as a lunchtime aperitif. A fresh fall of snow had blanketed the Oak's grounds. Not just a Xmas sprinkle, but an almighty February deluge. The sort that snuffs out schools, offices and churches and leaves behind a pure blank A4 in its place.

As they left the packed snow creaked underfoot and almost everywhere you could hear a musical trickle and drip as the noon-day sun began to thaw the icicles along the old buildings cascaded eves.

"So perhaps you should 'put on' as a doctor" Sandra almost sing-songing said. Dahlia eyeballed her with amused puzzlement. "How could you decide that I should become a doctor so suddenly?" Instinctively Sandra replied "because you look so loving and reproachful – isn't that what doctors are supposed to be like?"

They belonged wholeheartedly to one another – in their minds vastness there was no concealed corner that was not yet occupied with far more love than they will ever need.

Dahlia had always been a positive person, rarely given to depression and fear. Her anxieties had usually related to whether she could live up to what was expected of her. The maxim had been "Make the customers happy little girl. Keep your skirts up high and give them more than summer sunshine to fill their empty lives". Here with Sandra in the magic of the pre-dawn hours, lying together all arms and legs and breathing and listening to the rain and wind slashing around, she hoped never to see the sun again.

When Sandra was 17, to be pure and then to marry a pure man who respected you for being pure was the big issue. For Sandra, in those days, the world wasn't divided up into Republicans and Democrats or Catholics and Protestants or Black and White folk, or even purely men and women for that matter. Sandra saw the world as divided into people who had had sex and those who hadn't. This seemed to her the only significant difference between one person and another, but how to get started was the big problem. Mom had stressed in no uncertain terms to her that no woman truly knows about a man until it's too late. For example, a man's licentiousness was to try to persuade a girl to have sex by telling her how much they truly loved her and how they would marry her afterwards, but as soon after the girl had given in they would lose all respect for her and begin saying stuff life "if she would do it with them, she would do it with other men".

The one thing that Mom didn't tell her was what was

a girl to do? It had crossed her mind that maybe her partiality towards women was not so unbalanced as she had first inaccurately believed it would be. Withal there was a certain vulgarism about men and some sort of 'carry on' with a woman shouldn't be so confusing – should it? The more she ran it through her mind the better she liked the idea! Like the lightning and the tree, true love has no power to choose where or when!

Toto Riina's son Antonio's death went virtually unreported. The fact that he had endangered the Family's future to avoid conviction may have indeed been his stumbling block. However, whatever form of the 'Omerta' had taken it had been put into effect successfully. Therefore, it is not for me to enquire whether his 'Kisser' was slashed by 'cutting phrases' – I've no idea what to do with a metaphor in any event!

PART 32

'Oh-foi-de-roi' Shanghai Lillian

CHILDHOOD CAN BE an extraordinary time. Often it is a time of complex emotions, every-changing points of view and many cack-handed defeats. I guess that for most of us the particular aspect of our childhood memories are somewhat whimsical and enshrined in an imaginary landscape that, although sometime is boring, was nevertheless more than safe. However, for young Lillian Guerriri she sensed early on that there were some concealed actualities about her family that, although unfathomable, were nevertheless not unfounded. There was a certain sureness in the dark parts of the house, especially if you were hiding there and keeping your ears pricked!

At night ignore the fancy coffin and the boxes in the hall
We were only children
Children one and all

They do say that it's the small things that count when you are a child and it's the inches not the miles that will fill your memory as you grow older. It's true, the image of those small warm moments can be markedly significant, but what of the price to be paid when melanged and messed up?

Some folks died in mis'ry
Some of them in peace
They rarely died for nothing
But the dying didn't cease

After Cousin Toni and Valeria Guerriri ditched Lillian for keeps and moved back to Southern Italy and, not to be outdone as a 'participative parent', Lillian and I became quite connected. Lillian had always been an inordinately perceptive girl and it was heads-up that one day the barrel would have to be uncorked. She was needful for questions and she had a right to answers. Where did I come from? Why me? Who carried me into this time of day, away from whatever I don't remember?

I guess, to a certain extent, we pretty much exchanged notes – a quid pro quo of deviousness on my part as I wanted to get more than I was willing to give!

LILLIAN'S STORY

Lillian: I guess that one of my earliest recollections was of mommy Penny. She was always working on her old treadle sewing machine. It was pushed right up against the window glass so as she could get lots of light and also to let her look out and see the boats on the Hudson River.

I think of the time when I came home from school one day and recall her ripping apart (with relish) a red and white polka dot dress she hadn't worn in years. She remarked "Why, this fabric is just as good as new" pulling first one sleeve then the other away from the body of the dress. It was as though she was trying to interest me in her project and her practicality. Looking back on those days always conjures up a picture of Fractious and Maria always being close at hand.

The apartment gave the impression of being enormous with its high ceilings and long passageway; I guess for a kiddiewink it was. Mommy Penny had told me that it was a flour mill up until the depression. I was of the opinion that I was the most lucky girl ever – indeed I was mercifully thankful for my good fortune. You see, some kids' daddies worked in factories and some went to work in their Sunday suits and, although I didn't have a daddy, I had three mommies instead! When all of my mommies were home life had a new beginning and no foreseeable end, although it would start so quickly with Sandra and Dahlia's arrival and stop so quickly when they left.

For all the New York nights that ended before they really had permanence, to all the New York mornings that I awoke wondering how I could be nearer to Sandra and Dahlia – wondering what they wanted from me or expected of me so that I could be nearer to them.

How right it has always seemed to me to love them both across a room in our apartment, or across the seas and, if need be, across my whole lifetime. Without them I gain no understanding of any truth I may fall upon unless it has first been endorsed by them. Now, as I am becoming an adult, these kind of thoughts of optimism and trust frighten me. I am seeing the table bloody with red petals and I am understanding the little lies and the big lies and the reason and the importance of what you do and why untruths were told when there was no time or space to explain the truth. Lillian looked me in the face, appreciatively and with adulation: "If these words I have said to you have been strung out by me in such a way that hate by contrast may sound more beautiful, then it is only because I have been taught that love cannot always say loves name. I know that your eyes have been closed all these years and I wouldn't dare to have invaded your sleep. It's just to let you know that whatever time it takes, I have that time now!"

PART 33

Deigratia (By The Grace Of God)

THE CAT DOOR in the kitchen, all locked, blocked and boarded, looks so odd and out of place. Life has become less, less and less defined since the precipitous death of threadbare Fractious. No more stretched out on the cooling bathroom tiles, no more naps upon my desk no more 'sprinterlike' chasing of her imagination's moths.

I light one candle with another's flame and pass them along one by one to Lillian, to Penny, to Sandra, to Dahlia. Just a flea riddled compatriot, yet we miss her so much and her still curled as though sleeping and us, cold in the glowing candlelight of naked deathlessness.

It's strange how the outer reaches of the heart are often so profound that it becomes difficult to fully track them. However, I did see the outer limits of all of our hearts that horrible distant afternoon and for just once in my life I truly understood that the boundaries of sorrow are infinite. This new grief we all felt was wider than any reasoning. It was a desperation, a kind of condiment confirmation to the true psyche of our souls. Penny remarked that evening that what we had all undergone was "like what medals are to heroes". I think I know what she meant.

Somewhere in our attic a cricket and its kin are moving in, unpacking their bags and inspecting their new residence. Isn't it curious how often it is that directly after an interlude of death, a prelude to life insists it gets under way?

Nobody Dies Like Bogey:

... casual at the wheel, rain and wipers walloping away in a blinding rainstorm. The usual blonde doll alongside who Bogey knows has talked. The good old roadblock dead ahead – quick shot of the moll with a scream forming and a final endearing look from Bogey… "when they lay us out you'll look a lot prettier than me; you all in pink, me with the scar I was born with!"

Tough as Marlowe, sassing Eddie Mars – San Quentin, Sing Sing, Alcatraz; if Bogey had busted out or died in the slammer once, he did it a dozen times over. Even the smoke he pushed at you was really no hazard to your health at all.

However, Bogey can be reincarnated entirely on the silver screen as and when we feel his absence, but Fractious is going to pass into cat oblivion until kingdom comes. Ilsa though was just another dame when Rick clinked her wine glass and, although I truly loved Bogey, I am going to miss Fractious more.

– In Memoriam –
Fate lifts us up so she can hurl
us down from heights of pride
Viz: In a movie they live forever
But in real life they died…
…*'here's lookin at you kid!'*

PART 34

'I Can Still Smell The Fields Of Tobacco'

PENNY WAS PRACTICALLY convinced that there really was a Santa Claus when Dr Hymia Minsk began courting her. Hymia Minsk was a genuinely all right sort of guy. From time to time he would leave Penny surprise vest-pocket gifts tucked away under the davenport cushions or stuffed hidden in the toes of her shoes, or under a pleat in her clothes. Penny was like a neurotic child when Hymia was home and he never ceased his quirky wooing for an instant to her. Every so often when he was more than middling stocked with dinero (perhaps he'd just fulfilled a contract or such like) he would reward Penny with ten G's for every gift she found hidden away.

Penny really did love Hymia so much, although she had no false or unreal ideas regarding the background of Hymia's goodies. She more than realised that the diamond-studded vanity case sticking out of her stocking and all of the beautiful brooches and rings were not entirely 'incontestably' hers beyond doubt.

You see, Hymia Minsk was one of the 'old stagers' of which there were very few left, still drawing breath that is, and for all of Hymia's sins he was still second to none 'git em up' guys of all the amiable low-life in Lower Manhattan and Broadway. A certain amount of Hymia's more unpleasant jobs he would invariably leave until evening time. As he would leave our apartment to go about his leery obligations, I'd hear the dulcet voice of Penny hollering kind encouraging words after him. She would call out things like "think about my white panties darling" and "don't miss like last time" and "don't smoke, it's bad for your heart". The last 'pronouncement' was the only one that ruffled Hymia's feathers. "Of course I smoke, does she really find that surprising?" he told me. "Men of my age have always smoked, or chewed, if that was their pleasure!" Then he'd cock his sawed-off and pass into executioner's oblivion for several days. I liked Dr Hymia Minsk, he was indubitably and factually the most rascally son-of-a-gun of one kind or another!

In actual fact there is not too much I can say about the Crackerjack Ladies that I had shamefully become involved with, except that perhaps after a while you begin to acclimatize, to sort of get your bearings and at some point you begin to fallaciously view the whole ball of wax as both tolerable and decent, at least that's' the only explanation I can admit to.

Like several nights ago I decided to meet Sandra and Dahlia off the Toronto bus; they'd been to Canada on business. It was there that I found them both sat with their suitcases in the furthermost corner of the bus concourse building nonsensically bawling their eyes out. What could I do with crying women at the end of the line? – metaphorically speaking that is.

I took a serious expression like gander at the others folks in the terminus, just in case there may have been an incident and one of them had upset the 'waifs'. The guy next to me just shrugged his shoulders and two paraplegics on sticks – well they did nothing! I guess it wasn't anybody's business, or mine for that matter. It was a confidential matter between the two of them; although ten-cent to a dollar I'll wager it was an intractable issue that was connected with their work.

I knew that Dahlia and Sandra had a meeting scheduled at a doughnut shop in Scarborough, a suburb of Toronto (nicknamed 'Scarberia' by Torontonians). Dahlia had jokingly quipped that they were taking this so-called enforced vacation "to clean house for a pre-eminent figure". So the story goes that there had been hostilities between certain competing factions in Scarborough which urgently needed straightening. It was formally agreed that at least two trigger persons were essential for this particular job.

One of the thorny pricks in the Organisation's side was Quebec native Yves Trudeau. I knew Yves when we were both just striplings of around 17 or 18 years of age. We sort of lost contact after he joined a local Chapter of the *Hells Angels Bikers Club*. As memory serves, that was around 1976. I heard via the grapevine that he had boasted to being the very first Canadian to wear the Chapter's 'Filthy Few' patch which indicated that he had murdered at least once for his club. In actual fact he was involved in many more murders and finally when the law ultimately nailed him, he turned states' evidence against the Organisation. The guy was paroled during 1993 and was granted a new identity as Denis Cot'e.

I am pleased to say that I didn't know Griselda Blanco personally. However, for his part in my novel my brother

Mike did date her for a while because he was so, so hoodwinked into it. You see, Griselda was usually only sexually attracted to other women. Despite that, she and my Mike really hit the ground running from the onset. Said she would cut off both his hands if he ratted out on her. Mike was a clairvoyant so 'hands' were an essential part of his trade! He told me that he and Griselda shared the same cruelty, its meaning and its hydrodynamic – and how to apply them!

Variously known as 'Mama Coca' (you guessed it, cocaine was her thing) and La Madrina she was deemed as responsible for some 200 homicides and was finally indicted in 1993. However, she plea bargained by mentioning a respected member of the Organisation and got herself paroled!

I obviously didn't know Sam ('teets') Battaglia who joined the infamous bootlegging company led by Johnny Torrio and 'Snorky' Al Capone during 1924. By the way, he had earned his nickname 'teets' because in his role as Capone's collector of overdue accounts, he would threaten to "bust in da teets" (teeth).

Teets was indicted on extortion during 1966. However, his son Sam Joseph picked up the batten; mainly terrorizing restauranteurs and their employees. He should have had specified which ones and which people were a definite set controlled and owned by the Organisation!

All three of the above vanished following a meeting with their 'lawyers' on August 14th 1993. Some corpses were unearthed from a tobacco field just outside of Delhi, Ontario. The crime remains officially unseen and unsolved – in other words, no witnesses, no case! It seems to me that the informants risk outweighed their hopefulness and that kind of optimism frightens me of late.

For the better part of this week I've been out walking and come back and been out walking again trying to figure what the girls' tears were all about. If I were their preacher, their teacher or their Dad I could just go right up and ask them. However, although I am a 'double' friend, I am still a person so in need of my own self-adjustment as to offer help to folks in their line of work.

Having said all that, the only valid explanation I can come up with is that the fear for each other's safety may have been compromised on this last assignment and that their love for each other has a superiority that ranks above mere achievements.

Though on one occasion that evening I did discover ('unearth' would be a suitable word) that Dahlia, Sandra and Hymia had a familiar 'aura' about themselves. It was on the evening that they each returned home and we all sat cheerily around the table together anticipating the finger licking victuals that Penny was poised to serve. It wasn't really worth me mentioning it to anyone so I didn't. Nevertheless there seemed to be a distinctive smell of tobacco fields in our family room that evening.

I knew that rasping smell by heart. When Mike and me were kids we spent a couple of summers working in the baccy fields of Southern Ontario. It was such an absurd mockery really, inasmuch that we were far too young to legally purchase cigarettes and yet us and a bunch of other kids, as young as 7, were permitted to work the tobacco fields and to be exposed to acute nicotine poisoning!

Anyways, from the smell of it, perhaps my friends had all been out doin' some cuttin' and stacking or some such today.

But, like I said, it wasn't really worth me mentioning it to anyone – so I didn't!

PART 35

Butterfly Mornings And Wild Flower Afternoons...

IN THE TRANSFORMATION of life things must surely change – by definition we can't remain the same, can we? In the end are we not all dandelion seeds, blown away and lost in the endless firmament? If only that were really so.

There is no cluster or single day of my life with Dahlia and Sandra that I'd want to have changed or altered so far. Although possibly there were several days that I wouldn't have minded missing. However, I suspect that I could not have come down to this place where I am today in any different way. I suspect as well that being here doesn't necessarily imply that I know exactly where I am, because I don't.

It's not at all that I am afraid of what's likely to be upcoming or what blisterings have gone before. Indeed, what bothers me the most is how much of it is left – and that's what is critical.

Sandra says "Ricky, there are no answers".

Dahlia says "I'll make up some neat answers for you shall I?"

They are real treasures, always so sympathetic and kind-hearted. Even so, just for once I'd like to hear a brand new question to my answers, that's all!

"… catch me there
gonna get me there
if I have to climb all of the
mountains on the moon
I'll be in butterfly mornings
And wild flower afternoons."

Richard Gillis

PART 36

Annabel Lee And Me!

A BLACKENED WINDOW-PANED limousine slowly and unobtrusively trundled to a standstill outside of the main entrance doors of their apartment suite. Like a storm of ultraviolet diamonds let loose, Dahlia and Sandra quickly piled together into the rear seating clutching an assorted mess of ragbags and a surplus of cold water bottles. The driver's eyes almost staggered and toppled out as he gandered over his shoulder at them. Seems to me he may have had a fascination toward handsome ladies in suede coats and boots! Like two nippy, zippy sisters getting into chilly bed sheets they eagerly squeezed uptight together. At 6.30 in the am, it was much too early yet to consider yourself wide awake enough to become properly alive!

Out on the streets the first fall of leaves were lackadaisically flying across the frenzied emergence of September in the city and all of the things we didn't know we were looking for imbued us with a new sense of purpose. It's strange how the city can have that effect. It's as though it is our silent enemy, or perhaps just a hard to understand friend?

"In the people whom we love, there is, immanent, a certain dream which we cannot always clearly discern but which we pursue"

Marcel Proust

Seven years later it is hard to believe that I have shared such unutterable stuff with Dahlia and Sandra. Prior to that I spent most of my time staring into the same hole among the dead poets and artists that I revered. I believed that no other human beings could be absent yet give eternity like they were able to do. That was until my first encounter with Dahlia and Sandra.

So, once upon an autumn morning I extol every leaf being blown confoundedly across the city and those lying on the ground and filling public fountains and those catching in the gutters and diverting little streams of water and those who are banged about by brooms and trampled underfoot. Brown and red leaves, swirling bewildered leaves, September leaves, I extol you all!

At a great loss to my time I would dearly take pleasure in shaking out every single book I own just to find, to catch, to keep alive, to perpetuate forevermore those falling leaves this autumn morning, in this particular place, with these particular people.

I'd like to be a writer
But I am really undecided
Cause I long to be a cowboy
And my thoughts are so divided.
I don't want to star in some
'B' movie feature
I have a lot of black clothes though
So perhaps I'll be a preacher!

In the meantime though, here I am riding my imaginary horse down 42nd Street heading off with my partners on the trail to who knows where? That is the question I've been asking – where are we travelling to and what will be my role when we get there? Having pumped and quizzed all morning, the only big dollop of an indication they gave me was "it's nothing that is associated with killing or death!". A Sunday preacher in a cowboy hat, waiting for the next event – that's me!

Sometimes it becomes necessary to find out about 'things'. Sometimes 'things' can actually demand that you are told about them. It's a bit like having loose laces on your shoes that require tying up. How long are you supposed to be patient whilst they just 'flip flop' the whole time?

So, with that in mind, I was kind of relieved when the limo finally came to a halt outside of a rather abstemious building. There was a whole lot of activity going on as painters, glaziers and workmen crawled all over the place.

I remember Dahlia and Sandra mentioning this project some time ago. I didn't really give it much heed and assumed that, although it was an excellent idea, it was very unlikely to happen. How totally wrong I was!

Whether it's ego or the need to be understood, most of us go on forever attempting to redefine ourselves. I've tried often to do it in poetry. Sofas in time became davenports, victrolas became phonographs and finally stereo equipment. Although a milkman is still a milkman, it is very possible that this new venture may be the positive equal to happiness that Dahlia and Sandra need. I see no reason to disbelieve that.

The premises had been a former Sally Army hostel. I

guess the more 'well disposed' clientele of late found the East Side rather 'indelicate' and so in due course it closed and fell into disrepair.

They chose to name the spot *Chimes of Freedom* after a Bob Dylan lyric that Mom was especially fond of. It was inscribed in large lettering on the foremost face of the building. Expressed directly below, coherently and clear was the wording:

Women and Girls Refuge Centre and Workshop.

In a nutshell, this was a safe house for folks who were too afraid to unload their consternations and a place where they could learn some interesting sterner stuff as well!

"I always wanted to use the Mafia as a metaphor
for America"

Francis Ford Coppola

There is something about the poignance of a particular kind of ambition that sets out to do something risky – dare to say bold. I think that in many respects it's dated nowadays, almost nostalgic. Perhaps tragic? In any event, this was never going to be any paint-by-numbers exercise. It would either be the bravest failure ever, or possibly a massively flawed success!

My involvement was clear:

First and foremost I needed to pump up the volume on my supportiveness, but at the same time attain a certain hyperbolic balance between them helping folk and 'killin' folk! Perhaps a somewhat cautious double overkill in favour of them helping folk wouldn't go amiss! It may all sound rather schmaltzy, however, that's the way I see it!

I set up my own 'vest-pocket' publishing house in one of the unused larders. It was kind of dwarfy and windowless, however, it fit the purpose and was lovely and cool in the summer. Here I'd send out promotion dodgers (flyers), press releases and such.

Here is the central theme of them:

Think about this – women are fast becoming collaborators in their own demise. They are allowing themselves to be commercialized commodities that can be bought and sold – something that is useful only at the time it is useful and no more! The sad irredeemable truth is that ten, twenty or even fifty years later they begin searching for the person that they thought they were, but unrecognisably that person is spent and done with!

I think it was Elton John who remarked that he would go to bed with either a man or a woman, but drew the line at goats! It seems to me that the vast majority of 'traversable' individuals; women and gay men; will heedlessly settle for goats time and again rather than be not 'wanted'.

At least one out of every three individuals in a so-called relationship has been either beaten, coerced into sex or otherwise abused with the abuser usually being someone known to them.

"Equality of rights under the law shall not be denied or abridged by the United States or by any State on account of sex"

A misnomer perhaps?

In the United States the Equal Rights Amendment (ERA) giving women the same opportunity for advancement and earning power as men has not yet been totally ratified. Though most of us thought that the Bill of Rights had made it unnecessary for the ERA to exist?

An intelligible justification perhaps?

I guess there still are a minority of voters, both men and women, who truly fear that in the event that women are solemnly promised their unconstrained rights, they may therefore be obliged to bend over a hypereal jackhammer in the street!

Dahlia was social, loving, outgoing – in a word extrovert. After all, when she worked as a showgirl 'expression' was the core of her activities. She had dreamt up this concept of what she called 'protective posturing'. In many respects it was merely the beginning of 'real dance'. Nevertheless, it was Dahlia's formulative move to engage her novices in a close emotional relationship with themselves: to purvey some self-esteem in them! Pelvic tilts, knee presses, stomach presses, leg lifts and arm stretches were all power for the course and how to work correctly instead of painfully, that was all important too!

Now Sandra's contribution to 20th century music cannot be overstated. 'Juilliard School of Music' it wasn't, nonetheless the somewhat geriatric 'joanna' they came across in 'Four Corners' thrift store on 6th Avenue (bet. 13th and 14th Street) was a joy to behold (as reconditioned uprights go!)

Sandra's personal view of the way in which music is approached and appreciated is based upon fact and knowledge that she has earned. It was, therefore, especially intriguing to me when she alluded upon the reason why folks are so inclined to starve themselves of classical music. "They feel intimidated" she said. "It's like a foreign language to them." I confessed to her that I once wrote sixteen lines of a new overture to Don Giovanni. "It just walked up from my belly to my head" I told her. "That's when you know it's good Ricky" she replied. "You should have completed it."

Anyways, Sandra would fire up her gaggle of snapdragons clapping just the rhythm pattern of a short melody or such and then she would step it up until music was "walkin' up from their bellies" – that's just what Sandra did!

Annabel Lee

It was many and many a year ago
In a kingdom by the sea
That a maiden there lived whom you may know
By the name of Annabel Lee;
And this maiden she lived with no other thought
Than to love and be loved by me.

Edgar Allan Poe

Was Deborah Kerr really just an English rose?

What would Marilyn have been like in her fifties and sixties? Would she have proved adaptable?

Is Doris Day still trying to protect her virginity; if so, why?

Does Carolyn Jones (Morticia in TV's *The Addams Family*) often wear black so fans will pay tribute to her acting?

It's so effortless to ask myself these half-baked questions when all of the answers are equally as absurd. Be that as it may, I was introduced to a person who attended the Refuge Centre earlier this evening. Her name was Annabel Lee.

For reasons which I cannot determine, I appear to be getting way ahead of myself over Annabel Lee. The question that perplexes me a lot is, *why*?

PART 37

Lucky 'Lemonade' Lucy

IT SHOULDN'T BE that we keep past mistakes in our heads; it's just so unhealthy! It's not only downright neurotic to continue to think about them, it also unquestionably verges on psychotic to dwell, dwell and dwell about them.

However sadly so the past does often repeatedly stay with us and haunt us – probably because odds-on it is not even past yet. Unsuspectingly we may find ourselves examining again what happened and imagining the consequence of what might have been. Like gazing into a concave mirror of the past to try and enable us to see around the curves and to see ourselves. The horror of looking deep, deep into the eye of the storm and irrevocably discovering that you in fact were that 'eye'.

"We did it" Sandra declared "we did *all* of it" Dahlia added corroboratively. "This darn thing is not going to be a forum for us to discuss and dwell over" I told them sternly "so let's not do it, we owe that to ourselves—"

"Ricky's right" Penny cut in "let's move on."

Not that it really matters, but all of what follows is true:

Portella della Ginesta massacre

On May 1st 1947 during Labour Day celebrations in Piana degli Albanesi, Sicily, 11 innocent people were killed in what has become known as the Portella della Ginestra massacre.

Those held responsible were Salvatore Giuliano and his bandits, although their motives were never categorically established. However, papers found in 1989 suggest that Guiliano was in bed with the Sicilian Mafia. Giuliano's bullet-riddled body was found on September 6th 1950 and so perhaps we will never know all of the genuine story.

However, on the last days of his life Salvatore Giuliano paid a secret visit to the American Consul in old Palermo, offering to give them the staging-post for heroin into the US in consideration for relocating him and his pregnant girlfriend Marisa Maino into the United States.

The US Authorities still kept their promise and on October 2nd 1950, Lucky 'Lemonade' Lucy was born in the US.

Buffalo Daily News Today

Press Release

An abandoned vehicle belonging to Marisa Maino was found yesterday, three days after the blizzard that rocked the suburbs over the weekend. Police say that her disappearance is a mystery and would anyone who has information concerning the whereabouts of Maino please contact them.

It was forty-five degrees below zero the night she disappeared. In those conditions no one sees or hears a thing! I just knew that it wasn't going to be a set of circumstances where the police retort "Hi ... so you saw our note. Where've you been?" They knew that when a person of Marisa Maino's renown is gone, they stay gone forever!

"I recollect being lost in a snowstorm as a child.
Walking home, flashlight in hand, scattering
the snow with my tiny feet down the steep hill,
through the broken snow fence, through the drifts
to the doddery wooden bridge and crossing plank
by plank then disappearing into the bitter wind
that puffed up like smoke."

Ricky Dale

Lucky 'Lemonade' Lucy was in the ballpark of thirty years of age when her Mom 'vanished' – incidentally she got tagged 'Lemonade' because she was always on the 'wagon', and Lucky was attributed by her Mom, too bad Mom wasn't so lucky!

Lucy was part of a singing/dancing duet, the other person being her girlfriend Lola Sapola. Lucy and Lola had both trodden the boards since before Noah and yet they still had a genius to successfully draw in a crowd. You'd find them providing their cheery kind of entertainment most evenings, either at the Marx Hotel or the Crystal Room. A lot of the older guys, you know 40+ who had grown tiresome of their wives; without a doubt were really partial to them. For sure, Lucy and Lola had that kind of exaggerated burlesque type of attraction that made you erroneously think that they may take something off!

Sandra and Dahlia had become really chummy with them – exceptionally so when they first began to feel comfortable about making known their sexuality.

The connection between Salvatore Giuliano and Lucy's mom was something that Sandra and Dahlia couldn't have envisaged. It was a nightmarish sequence of events to cope with once they had fathomed it all out. If Lucy had not mentioned her mother's name on the telephone that night, Sandra and Dahlia would never have put the pieces together.

Penny was entirely right when she said we should "move on". However I thought that I might have a more amicable, if not somewhat ambitious, solution and Penny may be the answer!

My favourite American authors were Whitman, Dickinson, Isherwood, Sandburg and just about any author whose work seemed to me immediate and uncluttered. Penny's preferences were the same. I discovered that there was some kind of new excitement in her when we read Whitman or the others together. It was as though we both occupied exactly the same space. I don't mean to imply that she was somehow the best woman I ever knew; in fact to say such a thing I would be doing her a terrible disservice and a whitewash job on myself to boot! However, we did develop a surprising attachment toward one another and a rapport that I was unaccustomed to. Not in the beginning I have to say, it was kind of gradual and most probably began shortly after she left Georgia. So with all of that in mind, I intended to put forward a suggestion to her; and this is it:

I knew that Penny had a liking for the unused rooms in the loft space and yes, there was an unusual flavoursome ambience about them.

I was especially partial to the yellowy stained-glass panes that ran in a triangular design across the top of the windows. They buttered the rooms in a soft gold tinge like some innovative kaleidoscope might do.

Penny and I had a liking for spending time together up there, especially when the rain was lashing mercilessly upon the slated roof. There was something rather intangible about just sitting there relaxing, reflecting upon life and listening to the wind and rain doing their worse.

The hickory planked floorboards had long since soaked-up all of its precedents footfall and lay as if in deep sleep like antiquitous relics; except for a soothing musky permeation that seemed to ooze from within them and spread almost audibly through every nook and cranny of the buildings existence.

With the somewhat optimistic assumption that I perhaps may come a stone's throw away from success in persuading Penny and Dr Hymia that my suggestion was deserved of a second thought, Dahlia and Sandra advocated a 'back-up' plan. "We always have a back-up plan" Dahlia enthused!

Considering that I was inviting Penny and Dr Hymia to migrate to the 'pigeon loft', was I asking too much of them? Even though it is very very atmospheric up there!

Well my 'back-up' plan became the overruling tantalizer to quash all doubts. To wit, a wet room and Jacuzzi ensuite – that simply clinched the deal for us!

As it worked out, it wasn't really that difficult or problematic to nicely 'hassle' Lucy and Lola to live with us. They were gratefully relieved indeed to be offered Penny and Dr Hymia's former suite – great views of the Hudson too!

I guess it was chiefly due to a Buffalo County Sheriff's writ to take possession of Lucy's Mom's property. Evidently her mortgage payments and tax revenues had become delinquent since her disappearance!

Inasmuch that my plan didn't involve rubbing some poor soul out, or disposing of a cadaver, I really felt delighted regarding the outcome. However, away from this zany play on words, what was most gratifying was that all of my conspirators felt that it was a job well done as well. I think the fact that it kept all of us melodious 'academics' downstairs at a distance from the older folk was in all likelihood an advantage as well.

'Tis a great pity regarding Lucy's mom Marisa though … enough said already!

PART 38

A Deal With The Devil

"When inkpots are open and our words are nailed
We must then withdraw from our pursuits
With all the perseverance of a chameleon"

Ricky Dale

IN THE SUMMER of 1941, Mom Provenzano was holed up in a chic deckhouse on Philadelphia's Brandyriver creek. For the first time ever she was beginning to have a sense that she was not being properly appreciated and protected by the bosses of the Organisation. In due course they all grasped what Mom's intentions had been and realised immediately it was all a clear-cut misread misunderstanding. You see, Mom's folly was her antagonizing habit of 'going it alone' and sanctioning stuff without first acquainting the bosses of her intended plan.

Anyways, it all worked out well in the end. All the same though, what had caused the bosses to behave in such an anxious and agitated manner was when it came to their attention that Mom Provenzano was having a suspiciously long-drawn out get together with police and investigating magistrates in Washington DC.

In reality she had just staged the greatest coup of her life by getting Lucky Luciano released from his cell in Sing Sing in consideration of his collaboration with the US Government.

To enlighten you: the ultimate authority in NY docklands belongs exclusively to Lucky Luciano and the Organisation – through their careful manipulation of the Long Shoremens Union. During the summer of '41 the United States were fearful that Nazi saboteurs may endanger the docklands and cause widespread destruction to shipping. With that in mind there was no better protection than the Organisation. I guess that, patriotically speaking, in order to support one's country it sometimes becomes a necessity to adopt the strangest of bedfellows!

The US utilized Mr Luciano and the Sicilian wing of the Organisation again during the Italy invasion in '43 – not only did the US troops carry the Stars and Stripes flags, they also flew others emblazoned with 'L' for Luciano!

In 1961, completely out of the blue, I briefly spoke to Salvatore Luciano in the lobby bar at the Taft Hotel, NY (I'd first-nighted there and was returning to Canada the next day). We'd seen each other earlier in the evening across the road at Dempseys Bar so I said a friendly "Hi!" After we had exchanged names I asked him cheekily how it felt to be rescued by a sixty year old woman? His laconic reply was "She was a good friend – now get lost!"

An invaluable 'fixer' was what she was – that's what I reckon anyways!

PART 39

Plastic Silverspoons

IT WAS CLOSE by Thanksgiving Day when an unexpected RSVP dropped aberrantly through our letter box. It seems that the notable Rosaria Schifani was convoking folks to an informal soiree and would like us all to attend. Rasaria being the ultra-classy spouse of one of our very revered bosses; our subsequent acceptance was just as a matter of course.

Their NY residence was an immense penthouse apartment in Brooklyn Heights. The open-plan lounge and dining area encompassed spectacular floor-to-ceiling rose tinted mirrors all around it. The piece de resistance can only be described as a 'shop window' which promiscuously gaped out over the whole of Manhattan. These were people who indisputably had an eye for sensationalism: the breathtaking scale of which all rather terrified me!

Rosaria took her time and gave us a grandiose tour of their over elaborate 'crib'. Beyond doubt the most pseudo-poncey item I have ever seen was the 'his and hers' bidets, unexpurgated with gold taps!

Rosaria's taste was for oak, which combined together neatly with the tinted mirrors. Be that as it may, it wasn't a 'good oak' by any stretch. How would I know this? Elementary; I asked a *Canajan, eh!*

"Now, although oak has been Mare-Canized for decades, it just don't grow rightly in the Knighted States or the Briddi Shyles for that matter. Oak is naturally shy by nature and likes to hideout where there's plenty of wooder. That's why you'll find the most contented oak (hence the best) up around the Grade Lakes ie Spearyer, Urine, Mishgan, Eere and Untario. Together they form the largest body of polluted water in the world – and good oak loves that too!"

Of the 600 or so species of oak, not all are ideal for making furniture or laying flooring. I am astonished that Rosaria Schifani, being so acquainted with home finery and such, didn't know this key factor!

Anyhow it was all rather ostentatious for this homeboy's palate, I was easily out of my league. It was as though I had stepped into some quixotic bubble and somehow lost my sense of fathom.

Perhaps I was unwilling to accept that beyond the greenbacks and silk-stockings there could be normalcy and that all these ridiculous trappings of success were just par for the course? Or could it be that there actually is a liking to be professionally unorganised – could that be an oxymoron of sorts?

I have a great respect for Dr Hymia, however I do believe that of late he is becoming somewhat senile. Just tiddly odd things like, for instance, when he returned from work last week there were specks of blood all over his face and white shirt – not 'his' I might add! The other day I had to tactfully prevail upon him to change shoes

– he was wearing two lefts! I just feel that a gentleman in his line of work ought to avoid attention.

Not that it really mattered as such, but when we were first ushered into Rosaria's lounge, Dr Hymia strolled over to the mega-mirror to shake hands with himself! Penny realised immediately that he was confused and became the hand for him to shake!

In many respects Rosaria's soiree put me in mind of a 1960's type gathering. No one was smoking pot of course, but there was a lot of personal views regarding JFK, LBJ and Dr King. Rosaria obviously had a Dylan partiality who she irritatingly played on her surround sound over and over again – that really did hack me off!

We were introduced to two government guys together with their ill-matched female companions and a friend of theirs who does the Maxwell House commercials – she was very nice looking indeed! I have absolutely no notion of what the connection could be between them all and, to be frank, I didn't feel compelled in the slightest to ask!

It put the wind up me a bit when the hairy looking 'Boss' guy threw me a question. He only wanted to enquire whether or not I'd seen 'A Star is Born'? I replied that I hadn't yet seen it. To which he then suggested that I should and objectively added "It's all about a has-been rock singer like you Ricky". I think he might have been referring to the Kristofferson version, not the Judy Garland one; which had absolutely nothing to do with Rock.

At the end of a kind of absorbing evening there was an unexpected nicety to follow that wasn't at all wasted on our group. Just as we were saying our goodnights,

Rosaria handed Penny a real cute grey kitten. "It's an early Christmas present" she smilingly said. She also handed Penny two upper circle tickets to see the play *Heartaches of a Cat* at the Anta Theater. So I'm told, Penny straight away flushed them down the can when we returned home saying "It's a daft play – all the actors have animal faces".

In hindsight I guess it was a pleasant enough evening and I am grateful to Rosaria for inviting me. Be that as it may, I find the whole episode so untypically puzzling. Inasmuch that with all of the swanky opulence swishing around my head it is an insignificant image that dominates me the most:

Viz: The dozen or so plastic wreaths in a cardboard containable by their front entrance door – out of ten how often had they been handed down?

"Mama, put my guns in the ground
I can't shoot them anymore
That long black cloud is comin' down
I feel like I'm knockin' on heaven's door."
Bob Dylan, 1973

PART 40

A Phrase Of Love

'Stylized': 1

"It was many and many a year ago" ...

If there's one thing I have learned recently is that 'Reality' is oftentimes simply that oneself perceives it to be and nothing more besides. That being the case, would it not sound downright preposterous to have a shot at explaining or rationalizing another person's 'Reality' to them?

That concept would have been my unqualified personal view, verging on the morning of September 20th – several hours before my life was in collision with the life of the beautiful Annabel Lee.

"I was a child and she was a child" ...

The truth is Annabel Lee cannot reside either in my reality or hers for that matter. She is only ever going to find life in our combined fiction and it is here and now where my pen is put to paper in the only total honest way it knows.

"And this was the reason that, long ago" ...

Who is this person who virtually holds my humble pen with me: who writes with me in the way she wishes me to write?

Making me a character built into her reality by necessity – by sine qua non!

Making herself an irresistible presence built into my reality by the same identical emotion as mine.

"The angels, not half so happy in heaven" …

How indeed is it feasible that this person has begotten reality when I have not had the option of placing her in my fiction yet: she wasn't the one who created me was she?

Is she so confusing to me or so intentionally confusing me; or am I willingly allowing her to write about us as much as I let her?

"But our love it was stronger by far than the love"…

And now it's the moment to call it quits and move on from procrastinating the obvious. I no longer care that she knows little about me and I know little about her. The incontrovertible truth is that we know everything that matters about one another

"For the moon never beams without bringing me dreams"…

Wherever there are lovers laying on grassy banks beside blue rivers, or going upstairs to a thousand different rooms: I wish them all well; because I have found my blue river and my room; I have made fiction my reality. There is so much more now to me being myself and to her being herself too!

A Phrase of Love

'Stylized': 2

I RECALL SEEING Arthur Miller in Central Park one Saturday afternoon. It was quite a thrill just spotting him there straighter than straight, unvoiced, meandering along like a regular fella. I recollect thinking how very good-looking and refined he looked. A rich kind of Jewish look!

It's uncanny how likely it is to all of a sudden come across all manner of renown persons on the NY Avenues and thoroughfares. Like the other day for instance; I was busy doing my usual daily rounds of grocery shopping and such when I recognised a big guy with a 'funny' name. 'So, Organisation' I thought. That's when I chose to change direction and go the other way! It's not at all that I am fearful of those fellas, it's just that they make me feel 'uneasy', and it's not necessary! Folks with Italian monikers like Vincenti Risko, I avoid them or any one that looks like James Dean's dad for that matter! Which reminds me, I watched 'Rebel Without a Cause' several nights ago with my Annabel. She burst into tears during the part where the pint-sized Sal Mineo fell asleep and James Dean and Natalie tiptoed away to go kiss. "It was the thought that he was left alone with nobody" she said. "Why couldn't he have had somebody?"

Each time I watch that movie it never fails to bemuse me how Dean and Hopper are like grown men and yet they are supposed to be young adolescents. Dean, so modern, the jeans, Lacoste shirt, red windbreaker. "It's only entertainment" I tell Annabel and give her another Kleenex – and try to remind myself of that fact as well!

An erstwhile musician friend of mine decided to visit us whilst on a whistle-stop trip to Manhattan. His name was Jack Rich. Rich by name and pocketbook! Jack had been convincing people about this so-called infection he had in his brain for years. However, it was all baloney to gain sympathy and attention specifically from vulnerable young women. I mentioned it to Dahlia and Sandra who surprisingly were all ears. "He's working his way through the female Yellow Pages" I told them. "He started out with short girls and now that he has gained more confidence he's recently converted to tall blondes that are perhaps average looking. At the present time it's most likely tall Swedish looking beauties. I just bet it is! I guess he'll have another white baby with one of them soon then dump her for a tall black girl, right?

Jack abstained from 'trying it on' with my Annabel. She remarked that it was most probably on account of her 'wonky' left eye, but it wasn't. He did however allude to his partiality regarding our Lillian – her being blonde and somewhere between short and tall!

So the story goes, 'repairmen' Sandra Comanescu and Dahlia Carriera came to the rescue. Inasmuch they provided Shiatsu therapeutics to his scrotum and dispensed his sorry soul on a package flight back to London, England. I hear he's screwing black guys now – in every part of everywhere!

On a much more pleasant note, Dahlia invited the delightful Susan Sarandon to lunch with us last Sunday.

Susan and Dahlia had first met at stage school years ago, but had managed to stay in touch. She was great! She's a Liberal, an ex-hippie and she just talked her head off all afternoon – undoubtedly that's the type of people we adore!

We all (apart from Penny and Doc) trotted over to the Hard Rock Cafe during the evening. Regrettably that's where we lost Susan to an eager CNN camera crew.

It had been a brilliant day up until someone came in and informed us that Ricky Nelson had died in a plane crash in Texas.

I was totally shocked, I was such an admirer of him and how he had managed to stay in the limelight for so many years. Indeed he well nigh took over when Elvis was drafted into the military.

I remember how brother Mike and me used to identify with David and Ricky Nelson and would never miss the *Ozzie and Harriet* TV Show back in the 50's.

Annabel and me stopped and talked for a while in Union Square on the way home and I was in a kind of pensive mood which was unusual for me.

"Don't be sad Ricky" she said. "I can't imagine even you performing in a concert anymore either, let alone Ricky Nelson." As I groped for my cigarettes I thought "You know, she's right!"

ERIC HILLARD NELSON (Ricky)
1940-1985
RIP

PART 41

I Did – I Do

"And there will fly into the room
A coloured butterfly in silk
To flutter, rustle and pit-pat
On the blue ceiling"

Ivan Bunin

I LOOKED UP from Bunin's passage, wetting my lips as if to speak, but words wouldn't come. 'The girl has gone' I thought 'and darling that girl was you.'

It rained and rained and rained on the day of Lillian's wedding to a Cuban fella named Jerry Hall, who in appearance actually did resemble Che Guevara! Not at all related to the Texan though, who was married to Jagger.

His father was Greek and looked not unlike Telly Savalas in his 'Birdman of Alcatraz' role. They both hailed from East Harlem, somewhere in the vicinity of Dr Martin Luther King Blvd. I am told.

His Mama is pure unadulterated Italian hayseed and lives somewhere in Southern California. I thought she looked a smidgen like the great Joan Rivers. She remarried to a very serious Burt Reynolds type of guy.

Jerry's father also remarried but twice more. Once to a Chinese national who it was rumoured used to be Miss Taiwan. They had a son who is genuinely the very spit of Bruce Lee.

At present he is married to a nice Diane Keaton'ish Jewish lady. They have this ill-mannered little boy called Benjamin who is more than somewhat abnormally hyperactive and needs a good slap! In point of fact the Diane Keaton'ish lady had to return to her hotel – I think she had an infection in her tubes!

Jerry's Uncle Rey and his full-figured pest of a wife, Helena bullfrog, had flown in all the way from Mexico for Lillian and Jerry's nuptials. I liked him though he possessed a kind of distinctive aura, almost as though he'd just stepped out of some Film Noir double feature. A shazam brand, like Mitchum and Ladd, that I fear may never return. Uncle Rey read us all a particularly poignant passage from a Gideon Bible he had misappropriated from his hotel room. It was really apt, but straight away forgotten.

I really cannot understand why Rey's wife, the 'hairy' Helena, suddenly and unexpectedly developed an unearthly obsession to be with me. No matter how often I tried to excuse myself to go to the bathroom, she would just tag along and wait pathologically outside giving me a huge smile when I came out!

In 'Kiss Me Deadly' Cloris Leachman asks Mike Hammer "Do you read poetry?" He doesn't even answer, but just looks back at her and sneers. I guess the plot may be said to turn on a book of Christina Rossetti's poems, but to me it is that pause, that careless sneer on Hammer's face. He not only does not answer, but he sees no reason why he should!

Rey's enormity in life was shooting craps, that's what he did best and that's what he was doing. So no matter how many times I tried to grab his attention he would just look back and replicate that careless sneer, that careless Hammer sneer – Film Noir or what?

Don't you just hate it when people just obliviously cough and sneeze all over you? I'd been trying to avoid Helena's germs all afternoon, but they finally got me. There had been an amazing cornucopia of glorious victuals and attentive waiters, but I felt so poorly that I needed to slope off early to bed. Still I got rid of that Helena and watched Yankee Doodle Dandy on cable – so it wasn't all that bad after all.

Penny had told me she had received a letter from Cousin Toni and Valeria Guerriri several weeks ago regarding the forthcoming wedding. If you call to mind both Toni and Valeria cut and ran off to Italy when their daughter Lillian was still a newborn. Penny had passed the letter on to Dahlia and Sandra and by all accounts the Guerriri's were due to arrive at JFK last weekend. However, there was a throwaway mention that the Guerriri's had been admitted to an upstate sanatorium for the chronically ill – what a bummer!

The Courthouse was 'wildly' bustling with people, however the ceremony per se was in every respect spot on. Lillian was just glowing with all of the excitement. She looked so beguiling and yet so flawlessly pure at the same time.

She introduced me to an odd looking guy who said his name was Bob Dylan. He was wearing big dark shades and, to be bluntly candid, I really don't know to this day whether or not it was the 'real' Dylan.

Having said that, Dylan was never that 'real' for me

in any event. In my opinion he was merely a clever guy with an astute knack of mimicking 'real' people and by all account the amphetamines or such made it all sound right. I just never bought into that boy at all!

The only close shave we had was on our way to the Courthouse in the early am when we 'misplaced' Dr Hymia! Or at least he was not where he was supposed to be!

Penny eventually located Dr Hymia in the park next to our apartment. She said he was kind of impervious to all of the goings on and was just casually feeding his old bagels to a posse of pigeons.

After that she quickly had to rejig the leg length on one of my suits in order to fit the doctor. It seems that he had used a substance called naphthalene among his stored clothes to keep moths away. It was a real stinker and would not have been a pleasurable supplement to Lillian's big day!

Dedicated to Lillian

Dear Lillian
Thank you
For all the every days
That you made into holidays.

PART 42

'Stardust'

WHEN THE GIFTED composer Hoagy Carmichael collaborated with his elegant lyricists on the richness of the words to 'Stardust', did they unknowingly also have Georgia on their mind?

Viz: "a nightingale tells a fairy tale of paradise where roses grew."

Although the nostalgic lyric to Georgia is undeniably ambiguous enough to have an either/or connotation, the fact is that in 1979 it was unanimously adopted as Georgia's State song. I guess that there's no definitive Georgia belle, just many customised ones!

I love a song with a beautiful lyric that's somehow tinged with regret and has that unique rhyming with the heart as only music does. In whatever way or to whatever extent, it's all hinged upon what wretchedness the listener is undergoing and empathizing with at that particular time in their life.

I met the sultry singer Julia London years ago when she was a celebrity face for Marlboro cigarettes. I was a kid full of cockiness in those days and just out-and-out questioned her regarding the *Cry Me a River* lyric of the unique rhyming of 'plebeian'. Viz: "told me love was too plebeian, told me you were through with me, and." She was such a cultured lady and unfussily replied that the rhyming had been somewhat obscure to her at the time as well, however Arthur (Hamilton) wrote it, she added.

Straight lines were sometimes difficult for me to walk when I was a scrappy adolescent – good for little more than proving that at least I was sober enough to drive! Jim Bowie, Jimmy Carter, Ray Charles, Oliver Hardy, Martin Luther King Jr., Brenda Lee, Margaret Mitchell, Carson McCullers, Alice Walker, Little Richard, Burt Reynolds, Penny Penniman aka Bernadette Provenzano; home-grown as the Kennesaw battlefields are and reckoning that living anywhere else but Georgia is, ipso facto, like living in sin!

'The Song of the South'
– as told to Ricky by Penny (Bernadette):
"My dearest NY, all of your taxi horns have sounded their last retreat and it has become time to let me go. Beyond doubt you saved my life. When I was too old to run you steered me through the noisy crowds but, although you borrowed my heart, Georgia has only ever owned it. Manhattan, New York's gerrymander of tears. You taught me that neon's just as nice as afternoon sunshine and all twenty four square miles of it spoiled and convinced me for a while, but now the world I used to know has come along and separated me from myself and we'll be leavin' you behind NY – me and Hymia and Whiskers the cat are heading South!"

It's as though Bernadette didn't die – and she didn't did she? She lived on inside of Penny who was hopelessly hammering away to kill off the devout neediness of ever becoming Bernadette once again.

She looked at me over the top of her eyeglasses, a kind of shamefaced yet unrepentant look:

"It's needful for me to return to Georgia Ricky, if only to confirm that my endless hankering is not quixotic and that my night dreams of home are alive and patently abiding. Can you imagine how it feels to stand in the early evening mist? It arrives in town and gathers and darkens like a shroud – I yearn for that shroud!"

She continued – ad infinitum!

"Have you ever experienced a Georgia spring or fall Ricky, when everywhere is awash with the colour of azaleas, camellias and magnolias and then like, all of a sudden, the snow runs faster than was planned? That fine powdered Georgia snow Ricky. Perhaps I'm being a morsel over melodramatic because the signals that snow is coming are usually pretty good! In Georgia it just snows in such wild and dizzy patterns – whilst here in NY it is a quiet saddened snowfall, as though no one really cares about it or for it and just refuses to take note of it."

By now Sandra and Dahlia had returned home from some clandestine shebang and we were all listening somewhat attentively as Penny continued to pour her heart out:

"No one is critical about kids in Georgia, they are allowed to grow up in a natural way. I didn't wear anything but overalls 'til I started having the 'Curse' – my mom rewarded me with a handsome polka dot frock!"

"You can buy pomegranates and bread sticks at the store and roast your own taters in a hickory fire. You can skip the flattest stones across the silentless creek and suck the sweetness out of a grass root, and me and old Hymia can kiss in elevators or on the courthouse steps because no one will give a damn!"

Dahlia was pouring us all a 'sentimental' dark rum and coke just like Mom used to make. Two thirds rum and one third coke! Penny really had the room's attention now:

"Your grandpa ran a whorehouse just outside of Atlanta with great exactitude indeed. Six days a week were legitimate, but on the Sabbath them whores kept their drawers on and he would go fishing all day! When he eventually died all of the townfolk came to church to see him off including his whores, but they had to sit on the opposite side of the auditorium!"

"And what of Jim Crow Dahlia? Well he's stone dead too! That Civil Rights Act of 1875 specifically states that everyone, regardless of their colour or previous servitude, shall be entitled to the same regard – all Georgians, black or white, are good decent folk in any event; so we are!"

Dear Penny had been obliged to pay so many emotional bills during her life – what with her sister and all – that I could easily imagine her one day stopping at the heaven check-in desk and demanding a refund! However, that wasn't going to happen just yet because we all agreed that tomorrow we were taking Penny back to her roots … tomorrow that tiny bird winging its way past the morning moon on its way South would be her! Home to where the corn is remorselessly the colour of ripe lemons and the grasshopper laying non-violently in the tall grass is Hymia – and she his indolent butterfly darting from marigold to rose and back to him again. It's so true, Hymia needed to eliminate his need to eliminate, and now he can surely do that thing.

**I am going home
to see if there really is such a place
as home.**

Several days later Sandra hired us a flamboyant limousine and we took turns to drive Penny and Hymia to a cute little Georgia town named Chickamauga (their choice). Having booked them in at a nice but inexpensive lodgings we all picnicked on the bank of the Lafayette River in the Georgia sunshine.

Last I remember seeing of Penny and Hymia was of them splashing happy-go-lucky in the shade of the old Road Bridge (I'll never forget the sight of Hymia in his wet string underwear!)

Like a carefree mermaid and merman with no place to go any longer because they were both already there!

**There's a certain sureness
about home
that stops you asking
its name!**

PART 43

Pianissimo

And on and on we'll go.
Through the wastelands, through
the highways
'Til our shadows turn to sunrays
And on and on we'll go

THE AFTERMATH OF losing our close friends to pastures new was difficult at first to adjust to. However, by early October freshets of new energy and interest were beginning to engulf us all. Combining in a powerful stream of reinvigorated ideas our lives began bounding us along again at an ever-increasing pace.

For me personally, a major change was in my attitude toward matrimony which I'd consistently viewed as 'strictly for the birds'. Nevertheless, of late it was beginning to enter into my equation. I had never really understood the concept of becoming engaged to a chick in the first instance; that didn't fit in with my logic at all until quite recently when Dahlia and Sandra suggested to me that becoming engaged might be of great benefit to my way of thinking, inasmuch that it would invariably leave me room to escape final commitment! And so here I am, not hardly on a whim, thinking carefully regarding popping the question to my beautiful Annabel Lee, at last!

We had all just gotten over the most gruesome dribbling noses and coughs ever. I guess when five people are all living in close proximity of one another all of those hapless souls being unwell at the same time is something of an ill-effected pantomime/psychological drama at the very least!

Could Glinda the Good be good enough, would you think that she indeed understood enough to get a girl back to Kansas? … Sandra and Dahlia understood:

When Dahlia and Sandra first came up with the concept of a refuge centre for women and girls it was predominantly inspired and pursued only because their own self-delusion and overblown pretension needed to be served. Although that's how the idea came into being it certainly wasn't the way the idea was eventually formulated or the way that it is now.

What propels them now is the people themselves and their elastic response to everything that Sandra and Dahlia are attempting to achieve for them. When the people are as motivated as the practitioners, it kind of provides a bottomless well of new discovery from which they all can drink.

At first many of the quasi-social gatherings provided a mixed bag of 'guests'. Inasmuch that a good percentage were men – gay and otherwise. Sandra told me that many of them were just desirous of not being disregarded. She said that sometimes you could detect an edge of malice in their voice which saddened her immensely. However, like earthworms in a box, both men and women seemed to entwine genuinely and unpretentiously with one another – chatting away; it was as though each of them derived a kind of common sustenance from contact with the others.

I recollect the instance many years ago when I was a punk Cadillac salesman. I was newly wet behind the ears and foolishly imagined that my 'commission only' vocation selling Cadillacs could potentially make me very rich.

For about six months I lived on nothing but Coca Cola, dry toast and crackers and slept in an unfurnished lodgings on an uneven parquet oak floor. However, during the evenings after work the circumstances and surroundings seemed far less unpleasant because there were ten other unfortunates all sharing that room and sleeping on that same floor as me. I guess that, like the Centre, anonymity can be somewhat bane, whilst recognition of being in the same boat is an anointment of sorts – at least that's the way I interpret it!

That Christmas Dahlia, Sandra and me put on quite a lavish stage show for our people and their kids. My role as an unnoticed usherette was no great surprise to me, although I really did enjoy the show immensely – except for the part where the Witch of the North is offering Dorothy the magic shoes. One little kid was forced to choose between watching Dorothy or obeying nature and the kid opted for both at the same time! Dahlia jested that 'cleaning up' in dramatic settings in the 'Organisation' is a well paid profession that I should consider!

I was delighted by the early Xmas present that Sandra and Dahlia gave me. Viz: a small neat snub-nosed Smith & Wesson .38 calibre pistol (duly registered).

I'd been having regular weekend tutelage by a US Marine friend of mine. I practiced squeezing off rounds at isolated stumps and river rocks, but under recoil the wooden grip had begun to blister my palm. The girls thought that my milquetoastness was highly amusing and began to refer to me as 'Annie Oakley' for a while. However, my general comfort level did increase after they suggested I wear an industrial glove – which they thoughtfully procured for me.

A cool gusty wind was hurriedly stripping the mournful trees of their last dried leaves and sending the rumpled woolly clouds scudding aimlessly across the staunch sunless sky.

This old and surly weather had no difficulty in persuading me to stay indoors and perhaps attend to a few boring tasks that I'd neglected of late, like my suit pants that required realigning after Dr Hymia had to sequester them for Lillian's recent wedding.

I knew that Sandra and Dahlia didn't require my helping hand today. I think they were trying to divert the mood at the Centre by initiating some trendy 'leg art'.

I was kind of jolted to hear the front doorbell chime, nobody was expected and, to tell the truth, I didn't really care to see anyone today.

Standing obsessively close to the door was a fella of about my age in a 500-dollar suit. It didn't, however, disguise the fact that he still looked like a low life to me.

"Hi Ricky!" he said in a tone of false familiarity, "I've come to tune your piano."

I noted he carried no tool kit as had other piano tuners that had visited from time to time and, to be perfectly blunt, he didn't look at all the quintessential piano-tuning type to me.

"I have an order here somewhere" he said and started to reach inside of his suit. I had lived with Sandra and Dahlia a very long time and picked up on little details – most of no real significance to me. However the signs they taught made it known that the fella was reaching toward his perjurous shoulder holster and not his inside pocket!

The vision of my handgun sitting locked in the bureau drawer had been flicking through my head like a cinematograph, but I realised it was far too late to retrieve it now.

Sometimes you may not need a bear's claws scratches upon your frosted window panes to warn you that danger is close at hand and sometimes, as if instinctively, you may become aware of an overwhelming iron silence; a shivering, chilling silence that turns your blood to ice. It is only when your speechless lips become restricted and unable to even utter transparent words in lower case, it is only then that intuitively, without conscious reasoning, you will react and I deliberately did!

Perhaps it was the way in which the scissors lay there on the sewing table (oh the geometry of the scissors!) Perhaps it was the justice that the scissors demanded (oh may the will of the scissors be serenely done!)

In hindsight it seems to me that very few lessons are indeed learned through fear and I believe that almost certainly it's because each and every fear will always contain its own individual peculiarity. However, once you have ascended and dealt with that fear threshold, you may actually grow to love it. At least that's what I found on that staunch sunless day last October. Maybe Dahlia and Sandra too have found the self same thing.

I remember well standing there afterwards with the pinking scissors in my left hand as though I was off to prune the roses around the apartment, except that there are no roses in our apartment!

That evening Sandra loosely observed that the unfortunate stranger's odd visit was indeed puzzling. In particular the size eight lopsided brogues on his feet and his thick as ninepins bifocals. Dahlia frayed in with "Poor Yorick, perhaps he was a short-sighted freelancer?" "Or a Wacko!" Sandra added.

I guess it was rather an unpleasant end for the guy in any event – perhaps without reason; maybe he really was a piano tuner with a penchant for side arms and high-priced suits – or not!

It was nice to get out of the apartment later that evening. We drove out to a magnificently beautiful clearing somewhere down river of the Hudson. We'd often go there on summer rambles when Lillian was a child. The tide was perfect to lose all trace of the day's inadvertent happenings and that was all that I cared about at that moment in time.

Sandra and Dahlia brought along what they referred to as "severance drinks", specifically Gin and 'IT' eg 30ml gin, 30ml sweet red vermouth.

Sandra diligently shoved the wrapped up cadaver out into the murky water and we all toasted him as he bubbled away downstream.

I guess in many respects the experience kind of

moulded and transformed my perspective on what is likely to happen when you least expect it. In any event it was certainly a descent into a new and enigmatic phase in my life that is not meant to be understood by anyone but me though.

PART 44

Eschewal

AFTER THE RECENT happening Kim's counsel was most specific:

"The geezer you navigated through the Hudson is proof positive that somehow your anonymity has been jeapardized. I need you to vanish whilst the source of the obstacle is located."

I guess since Mom's passing there have been 'transgressors' – the 'Organisation' v compliance has always been a complicated issue!

However, one thing you can be sure of, people grow old, people grow tired; they forget. What may seem like a major headache today can become miniscule the day after. For example, when Dahlia and Sandra previously visited London, England during June 1982 the body of Roberto Calvi was found dangling from scaffolding beneath Blackfriars Bridge. Although the coroner's court pronounced Calvi's death as suicide, a further enquiry agreed he had been murdered.

Having said all that, a briefcase which Calvi had in his possession on the day had reappeared recently – although only briefly. Documents in the case unequivocally linked drugs trafficker Franco Di Carlo to the murder – inevitably Di Carlo's body was found eventually in the Thames. Thanks to the combined efforts of Blondy Swanson and

Uncle Mike it surely took the eggnog off the face of Dahlia and Sandra – and Pope John Paul for that matter!

Isn't it quick-witted how the process by which most North Americans can gradually lose all capacity for moral indignation can begin virtually immediately? Within an exact period of 60 minutes after receiving confirmation of Calvi's closure, Dahlia and Sandra had not only purchased BA tickets to Heathrow, but also had earmarked to view a beautiful houseboat moored adjacent to Regents Park and Primrose Hill!

I pray that I might never be hoodwinked even once again because it's God awful. Not possible? I know. Then I pray that we all find what we're looking for soon. I guess I thought it was my responsibility to sort out loose ends, inasmuch that Dahlia and Sandra's departure had been lightning fast. The Refuge Centre was my main concern and I hoped that Lucy and Lola might want to become involved, but were they pragmatic enough?

What colour should I dye my hair? Which perfume should I use? What kind of flower should I place in my vase? What colour beads for my necklace? At certain times Lucy and Lola leave me feeling so tired. If they begin to tell me stuff through breakfast it leaves me dead for the whole day! I mean drained clear down to my core. It's as though they are speaking a slimy ooze that tells me there's no hope of ever getting through my toast and coffee, let alone the day's events!

Perhaps I need to take a good hard straight look at the whole situation. I don't want to be influenced by their warped little outlook on life, but what if my outlook is skewed too?

The truth is Lucy and Lola are semi-intellectual artists who love all kinds of popular culture where the common run of people gather. Hold on! Perhaps with that in mind they did stand a chance in making the Refuge Centre a success. I am having a dizzy rush – I think I am beginning to feel alive again!

I watched them dancing, rubbing up against one another, the radio blaring and the air conditioning not killing the humongous humidity in the slightest and then, bit by bit, they stopped dancing and were looking at me kind of lasciviously, smiling as though they had just read my mind.

"Yea, we've already had an in-depth discussion with Dahlia and Sandra regarding the Refuge Centre – so you can fill our empty glasses now!"

A two month span in London, England with Annabel – call it vacation or escape? It can be a sorrowful experience how memories of home can weigh a person down. Like tiny precious stones the awesome reflectiveness of home heightens and intensifies the whole horrible inconsolableness of distance.

*

Letter to Lillian November 6 7.30am:

Our Dear Baby

Remember all of those strange things we collected together on Dead Horse Beach (aka Bottle Beach)? Half a pair of eyeglasses, a tiny mug, a glass medicine bottle and a whole school book satchel of horse bones which you insisted on taking home! Can we go back for more soon?

We wrote this poem for you darling:

The English sun is rising
In rich golden tones
As you sleep
Our day is starting
In a cool breeze
As you dream
Our love is with you
On the wings of the nesting birds
'Til you wake
And tomorrow the sun will rise again
And our hearts will be with you there
Each day we look forward to when
We're with you and those days we'll share.
Forever and a day
Dahlia x and Sandra x

Perchance The End

Chapter 1

Paternity

IN THE CROWD stands Mackie Messer – aka Mack the Knife. He's never asked and doesn't tell why so many lost their life … and whose assailant, still at large Mackie how much did you charge?

*

To be considered slightly crazy in the Organisation can be a major achievement. However, there may come a time when your elders are speaking in whispers and the stench of corpses begins to get up everyone's nose. It is then that odd things start to happen …

… Jenny Diver, Suky Tawdry, Lotte Lenya and Lucy Brown; add Linbergh Baby, Valentines Massacre, even the disappearance of Jimmy Hoffa and not overlooking Louie Miller as well!

I guess, dependent upon who you've pinned your hopes on, they are all par for the course, inasmuch their demise is not good, but it is as normal as you would expect!

Be that as it may, you don't meddle with the Chief Justice of the United States Supreme Court – no siree, that's like eating coke!

I guess that Salvatore was a born in the bone killer. In any event he seems to have been drawn to death at a very early age. Maybe it came from growing up with an intemperate family in the wood of Minnesota. I can imagine that would install a certain sense of unrestrained behaviour in anyone. In his later life the cold-bloodedness that permeated all of his executions evoked a great sense of terror in folks by just hearing about it. It was as though he had not one ounce of pity or sympathy in him for any of his misfortunate prey.

Much of the material I gathered about Salvatore came from chitchat and conversations I had with a carefully chosen assortment of his old buddies rather than just mere acquaintances. Of course I didn't approve of his line of work, but on the flip side he was doing it devilishly well, at least most of the time!

I edited out some of his buddies observations about him to a large extent because their views interfered with plain common sense. Inasmuch that the generous almost hero worshiping picture they oftentimes painted of him just wasn't that appealing to me at all!

Returning to my comments regarding the Chief Justice of the US Supreme Court – it was several years ago now that I really received some lessons in disillusionment relating to the sanity of Salvatore. Viz: a rough draft of an FBI report had come into my possession which confirmed to me that he was completely off his rocker.

By all accounts he'd been given a Richard Nixon's enemies checklist and was going ahead to expedite it. I also listened to an audio tape of him laconically sighing "Nixon's a lousy politician but I'll bite the bullet and do my bit". That's just the way Salvatore was – nothing was too much trouble!

He'd been determinedly rising up through the ranks of Detroit's 'Sugar House' Organisation when I first learned about his rip offs. To many he had become to Detroit what Capone had been to Chicago. In fact Salvatore's pedigree went back decades to the prohibition era when hooch was lucratively shipped across the river from illicit factories in Canada.

It was only because of Salvatore's time-honoured family tie, in that considerate efforts were being chewed over by senior figures in Detroit and Canada, to convince Salvatore to reconsider his 'Nixon' assignment. It was as though he didn't want to get off the hook and just played deaf!

I guess the Detroit river had family ties for Salvatore – he and et al had crossed it many times. Having said that, less than 10 days after an attempted assassination on Nixon's chief negotiator, Salvatore disappeared into the black water without waves, without wind, without sails!

It was all simply a matter of time before Anthony Salvatore Casso finally received his behind schedule comeuppance and someone punched *his* card.

If you care to read on, you'll most likely arrive at the same standpoint as me.

Salvatore was a journeyman of sorts – an avaricious 'gun for hire'. He not only had strong connections with the Sugar House Organisation in Detroit, but also he was a close associate of Mom Provenzano and Kim Comanescu – and the Bonanno family in NY for that matter!

The whispers were out that he had wives and offspring all over the shop – Central and South America, New York State, Canada – he just scattered his seed wherever he went. None of the so-called wives supposedly were aware of his supplementary activities or the precise nature of his business so everything was hunky-dory for him.

It seems to me that for honeyed decades Salvatore had been, for the most part, playing the role of someone else. Someone who he was the opposite of. As time went by it went past the point of just pretending – it was as though he refused to accept that the role he was playing wasn't really him at all.

The psychological effect of this kind of almost 'method' acting must have at some stage encroached upon what was left of his sanity – psychotically so!

Is it somewhat unstable (or unstabling) to act out fantasies and assume the persona of the person you would like to be?

Unstabling: My buddy Vince imagined he was Robert Mitchum after watching the WWII movie Gung Ho! Vince even joined the Marines so as he could act out being Mitchum – Vince's pop had to buy him out after only 6 weeks training!

Unstable: More recently a fella I was introduced to truly believed he was 'The Fonz' – didn't look or sound anything like him or Henry Winkler on a bad day! I cannot recall Fonz having a caliper on his leg and walking with a pronounced limp, can you? 'Happy Days'!

Perhaps being someone else is all down to 'spontaneity' and nothing else besides – and it's all Stanislavski's fault in any event!

Kim had secretly known about Salvatore's marital shams, but had decided to keep it under wraps. It wasn't that she was being sneaky it was because it was in the best interest of her family. After his disappearance she felt confident that no negative results would arise from the truth being told.

It was known by many people that Kim was single-minded when it came to the protection and well-being of her girls. Them not knowing the truth was no longer an option for her and whatever they were to find out, she knew they were ready for it right now.

Kim had lived in a rest home for several years – which I shall call 'happy rest'! From the outside it was a depressing looking dark foreboding type of building. Set among several acres of weeds and dead trees it looked as though it belonged more properly in a Gothic novel. Squinting through my windshield as I pulled up outside, I could easily imagine a girl in a purple dress on the edge of the cliffs and the old house in the background with its shutters banging!

However, once you stepped inside there was something rather endearing and enchanting about the place and it was handsomely furnished to say the least.

Kim was awaiting our arrival in the snug and welcoming lounge. It was difficult not to notice the uneasy apprehension on her face. "Welcome home to Canada my darlings" she perked.

I guess we were all moderately gutsy individuals and, with that blueprint in mind, it wasn't long before we were all calling back old images to make sure the evening came out right!

KIM'S STORY

In Sicily the mood is very bleak. After all Salvatore Casso used to regularly be pointed out to visitors on the streets of Palermo – like he was a superstar or some such. The only people who refused to know who he was were the police!

Kim continued on until she met herself coming round again and then hesitatingly she began to broach the subject she had been heading toward. She needn't have worried, when she ultimately reached the finishing line and passed the mace to her girls – they had always been capable of learning things 'pragmatically'.

DAHLIA'S STORY

An acquaintance of my mother told me my father was of medium height, dark and Latin looking. Claimed he was already a married man, but my mother was totally smitten on him so it didn't matter.

I remember him slapping my mother around a lot and then her one day leaving hurriedly with a preacher fella. I don't remember how old I was at that time. In one of the photographs mother had taken around the time she left, I am dressed in a sailor suit. There is a large arm wearing cufflinks reaching out and holding my hand in one corner of the photograph. I think that may have been my dad.

The name Todd McQueen springs to mind. My dad embellished Todd McQueen's face after he used 'nigger' to describe my mother.

SANDRA'S STORY

I remember he looked well-to-do. You know, gold cuff-links, tiepin and such.

Mother said he was from back East somewhere. He'd often stay with us, although I had a hunch that he was just passing through. When he was gone mother became a quiet drinker and the longer he was gone the more she drank. She never became aggressive or angry because of it, just sad. When mother died it was from a kind of cancer. The doctor said it was not commonly known in women until they started smoking heavily. She didn't die from drink though.

My father never returned after she died, but I've often secretly imagined him as being like Tarzan or Clark Gable or a Paul Bunyan-like character out of the North woods.

*

It was a dream evening, although the daiquiris played a big part too. I recall Hemingway saying "felt, as you drank them, the way a downhill skier must feel – like running through powdered snow." I think we'd all concur with that!

At the end of it all I thought how uncanny it was that all three people remembered that man the same way, which brings to mind a kind of quirky nicety I remembered from the very first get together that the girls and I had. Viz: they asked me if I'd mind helping them wrap the presents they'd bought especially for Kim – it was Father's Day!

From what I've heard regarding Salvatore Casso, he wasn't an ace father by any stretch. Had I been around when Dahlia and Sandra were little kids I'd have meticulously spelled out their dad's name for them in a word they'd understand:

D-A-M-P-H-O-O-L!

ADDENDUM

WHAT PAWN SHOP of the mind can possibly index all of the idiosyncrasies of all of the intimate buddies who gave themselves to me; without invention or restraint? For that, I still remember you and love you and dedicate this addendum to you.

*

She had a voice that was soft and gentle; a clean cut Southern accent that was very nice indeed.

Except perhaps when she became overly excited by having put the zing on somebody! That's when she is fond of using that beautiful voice a lot more than somewhat. Inasmuch that Penny loves explaining things in unlimited detail to anyone who will be attentive any time she gets the chance!

*

With his winter just beyond the hill for some time, it seemed to me that Doc must have an angle. And he did! With enough of Penny's Junoesque shape left to interest him, Doc's happy days in the sack were an outcome made certain!

*

They characterized themselves as being 'stage actresses' – a karmically balanced aphorism of sorts! I fondly call to mind a ditzy lady-love of mine who danced nonchalantly around the bedroom in her underwear. That's unerringly what Lola and Lucy do on stage – oh, and warble their heads off at the same time! The punters consider them 20th century Shebas from the neck down. However, they are not doing too bad for two girls from Newark, New Jersey!

*

One day she was just a child away from becoming a rattle-headed teenage adolescent. Then one day when I snoozed off briefly, I awoke and 'one day' had strikingly melted away.

Looking back at her changing moods and faces I find it hard to believe the beautiful woman that she has now become. There, there, there Lillian my itty oddleums – da, da daddy is here, I've memorized the words and have not written anything unpleasant about you – how could I?

I do believe that there is nothing more restful to the male eye than a gal with black hair – because it is even money that black is the natural colour of her hair! It just seems to me that gals will change the colour of their hair to any colour of the rainbow, except black! Why that is, nobody knows apart from it is just the way gals are. Dahlia Carriera was no exception.

*

She was unquestionably one of the great beauties in her day and while that day is by no means yesterday, or even the day before, she still holds on pretty well in the matter of looks! I roughly calculate that she is around thirty six or thirty seven, however, she still has plenty of zing left in her step and Sandra Comanescu's hair remains very blonde, no matter what!

*

Says he comes from the best family in New England (likely the worst in Old England!) Tall and rangy – built like a first baseman; has bleach blonde hair and an enormous appetite – that's Uncle Mike!

Few angels have been heard to sing hosannas around these lamentable ladies of diversity. I guess that when all is said and done they are not such persons as any eagle-eyed guy would want to become schmaltzy over – without perhaps mentioning it first to his lawyer, or the FBI! Sisters of mercy they are not, but in spite of that Mom Provenzano and Kim Comanescu are much more dependable and stunning than all of the stars in a California sky.

*

He mixes his words like coloured playing cards; he believes rigidly in bad omens and he is mercilessly searching for the moron who snatched the handbag from the elderly lady in the basement apartment and the limo driver who splashed and dirtied the blind kid's clothes.

A flower of death with unique difference, that's Blondy Swanson.

A fella can lose his edge when he hangs out long enough with such solicitous associates. He is apt to get to thinking that he is safe and secure from what may lay out there in the shadows.

First thing you know, along comes a contender with a blackjack and biffs him on the noddle just to show him how safe he really is! Apprehension and RD were always well-travelled companions.

Ricky Dale
A Profile

ONE OF THE most endearing characteristics about RD's penmanship is his natural ability to consistently give it an honest voice.

"Intertwining harsh reality, together with figurative fiction, whilst at the same time being objective and guarded is a facet of my writing that can be emotionally exhausting" he says. "I suppose in a way I am trying to gain my self-fulfilment through interconnections in my protagonists lives. Perhaps it's my unconscious effort to reinterpret events so that they fundamentally remain the same as when I witnessed them."

Ricky was born in the appallingly blitzed city of Plymouth, England although he was primarily raised in West Africa and subsequently Ontario, Canada.

"The British colonial governments didn't recognise responsibility toward educating children in West Africa and so I would occupy my time reading, writing and routinely singing pop songs to my Mom."

"Even before we'd heard about rock n roll we'd often 'slang dance' with the locals – it was pretty close to what rock n roll became."

"The European contingent in West Africa would get together fortnightly to watch the current newsreel at an army base. I recall watching a news item about a singer named Johnny Ace – made quite an impression on me at the time."

After returning to England for a stint, Ricky relocated to Canada this time. "I'd done some quite commendable singing dates whilst in the UK and so upon my arrival in Montreal I got some publicity shots which immediately hooked me back into the system."

Faking his age in order to accept nightclub gigs, Ricky quickly became a regional hit. Although he says some of the venues were far less than glamorous, the seedier spots did help to move him along into recognition.

Late one life-changing evening Ricky received an unexpected telephone call from Rudy Parker, manager of the fabled Brant Inn on Burlington's lake shore. Their resident band singer had a throat infection and Ricky was asked to cover. That evening he attracted attention of the owner, the now legendary impresario John Murray Anderson. A twelve-month engagement as 'second' vocalist followed.

"A kid with amazing stage presence"

John Murray Anderson.

It was still the era of big bands at the Brant and Ricky's soulful vocal style suited the Brant's sophisticated clientele. Although Ricky had provided vocals for Guy Lombardo, Stan Kenton, Les Brown, Harry Waller and other fine orchestras, his heart was always with popular teen music rather than dance and jazz.

"During my stay at the Brant I couldn't help notice that kids were playing Ronnie Hawkins on juke boxes all over. Ronnie actually haled from Arkansas, although he'd been adopted as Canada's own!"

It wasn't long before Ricky had formed his own band "and we were four-fifths Canadian!" he says.

"We believed that Ricky Dale and the Detonators could really give Ronnie and the Hawks some serious competition – we used an additional gravitas too, we were drenched in echo!"

One day out of the blue Ricky put his career on hold indefinitely after his childhood sweetheart became severely ill. "She was suffering from the pregnancy-induced condition toxemia. We couldn't afford adequate health insurance cover and so her condition wasn't detected early on as it should have been."

"By the time she had been nursed back to health I'd gained a lot of new perspective" he says. "Although my limelight moments had come and gone, I hadn't expected my popularity to last forever in any event."

In due course Ricky decided to return to his roots in Devon, England. "I was determined to try my hand in business this time" he says.

During the succeeding 22 years he pioneered as MD to three innovative companies located in Torquay, Falmouth and Weymouth.

Of late Ricky resources his time between his children and writing novels.

Acknowlegements

In addition to my publisher I owe special thanks to:
Dr Kimberley Jayne
and
Gareth Lee
for all of your invaluable encouragement
Special thanks as well to my new best friend
Karoline Stanton
whose meticulousness ultimately brought my novel
alive
I am indebted to you all
Ricky Dale

Also by Ricky Dale

Poems (1977)
Limberlost
Limberlost II The Legacy
Limberlost III The Prequel